THE MAID'S WINTER WISH

DAISY CARTER

CHAPTER 1

The West Country, England - 1864

"WHAT ARE those wretched children up to now?" Gladys Ebworth's eyes narrowed with irritation. She peered through the window to see who the culprits were, before slamming down her pen in disgust at the sight that greeted her. "I might have known it would be those two," she muttered. Pausing to look in the small mirror that hung by the door, she straightened the plain snood that held her mousy grey hair in place. "This is their final chance...taking advantage of my good nature." She continued muttering to herself as she strode down the corridor, determined to put an end to the sounds of merriment that had interrupted her from taking a count of the second-hand dresses that had just been delivered by the charitable ladies of the parish.

"Look, Florence, if you stick your tongue out and catch the snowflakes it's like eating sherbert sugar." Dulcie Pickering took her friend's hands and the two girls twirled through the fast-falling snow that had already settled several inches deep in the courtyard of Chalsworth Orphanage.

"Since when did you know what sherbert sugar tastes like?" Ten-year-old Florence giggled as they span even faster, kicking up clumps of snow with her boots. "Lean backwards," she shouted. "Close your eyes and let's pretend we're ice skating on the river."

They skidded and swooped, arm in arm, shouting with giddy excitement and oblivious to the shadow of matron scowling through the window.

"Matron's coming, Florrie, scarper or we're in for it." Ethel Worton hissed her warning and heaved the towering basket of dirty sheets into her spindly arms. She averted her eyes from matron's steely gaze and scuttled towards the laundry room, knowing that associating with the other girls would lead to another night of missed dinner and gnawing hunger. She liked Florence and Dulcie, but even at six years old she knew it wasn't wise to get too involved with matron's least favourite residents at the orphanage.

"Stop larking around this instant and get back to work." Matron's voice rang out, slicing through their laughter. The younger children who had gathered to watch melted into the shadows, hastening back to their chores, leaving Florence and Dulcie exposed and alone at the centre of the courtyard.

"Sorry Matron, we got carried away." Florence felt the familiar lurch of fear in her stomach every time matron's shadow fell over her and she inched closer to Dulcie for courage.

"It won't happen again, Matron. We thought the snow looked so pretty...the way it's like diamonds falling from the sky...and it is nearly Christmas..." Dulcie's words petered out as she realised that appealing to matron's festive spirit was a futile strategy.

"Are there some extra jobs you would like us to do? We finished polishing the floor a few minutes early, so we thought you wouldn't mind us getting some fresh air. I remembered the vicar said fresh

air is good for us in his sermon a few weeks ago."
Florence was snatching at straws, but she
wondered whether mentioning the vicar might
remind Mrs Ebworth of her Christian duties and
play in their favour.

"Are you taking the name of the Lord in vain,
Florence May? I always thought you were a wrong
'un, and you've just confirmed my suspicions." Mrs
Ebworth reached out, faster than a striking snake,
and clamped her meaty fists around the girls'
upper arms, almost knocking them over. "There's a
word for girls like you two...troublemakers...the
pair of you. I won't stand for it."

She frogmarched them back inside and
propelled them briskly towards her office through
the echoing stone corridor.

"Please Matron, we didn't mean to enjoy the
snow. I promise we'll do better next time, we will,
won't we Dulcie." Florence's plea came out as a
squeak but all it did was stiffen Mrs Ebworth's
resolve.

"You should have thought of that before
neglecting your duties, girl. It's no use begging me
for another chance now...the harm is already done.
How am I meant to keep the younger children in
order when you set such a bad example, tell me

that?" Matron thrust the girls out of her hands, sending them sprawling to the floor. She put her hands on her hips and looked at them impassively, as though they were little more than pair of ugly vermin to be swiftly dealt with.

"Would it harm to show the little ones a bit of fun now and again?" The words burst out of Florence's mouth before she could stop them, and she scrambled to her feet, tilting her chin upwards in defiance. "We're the ones who hear them crying themselves to sleep in the dormitory at night, not you in your cosy bedroom. Why is it so wrong to laugh, anyway?" Her frustration at the injustice of matron's accusations spilled over, making her brown eyes glitter with resentment. Matron was so charming and friendly to the other parishioners when they went to church every Sunday morning, telling them all how delighted she was with the children in her care. But as soon as they were back within the confines of the orphanage, and safe from prying eyes, her cruelty knew no bounds.

Dulcie scrambled to her feet and stood next to Florence, holding her hand. She looked up at matron's face where two angry spots of colour had appeared on her cheeks. "Florence didn't mean to speak out of turn, Matron, we know how hard you work for us" she whispered. "What we mean is that...is that...we'll try harder. Please don't send us to the shed tonight..." Tears gathered in Dulcie's eyes and she tried to blink them away. Crying always seemed to enrage matron even more. "Why don't Florence and I go and finish up in the laundry room. Is there anything extra you'd like us to do?"

Matron crossed her arms and glared at Dulcie. "I know what you're trying to do, but it won't work, I can assure you. No dinner for either of you and you can both spend a night in the shed. You can use the time to think about setting a better example to the rest of the children, can't you." Her lip curled with disdain as tears started to roll down Dulcie's grimy cheeks.

"Of course Matron, whatever you say." Florence squeezed Dulcie's hand, trying to reassure her. "We'll present ourselves at six o'clock after we've cleaned the laundry coppers and scrubbed the steps."

Mrs Ebworth looked Florence up and down, trying to decide whether the girl was being repentant or presumptuous.

"I only said that because that's what you asked us to do last time we misbehaved. Are there some other jobs you'd prefer us to do?" Florence asked innocently.

"Don't start that butter wouldn't melt in your mouth act with me, Florence." Matron strolled to her desk and picked up a ledger, flicking the pages over until she found what she was looking for. "Let me see. Ah yes, ten years old both of you. What a sorry week it was when you were dumped on our steps just a few days apart," she sighed, shaking her head. "Ten long years I've taken care of you, and still you torment me almost every week with your insolence." She snapped the book shut and studied them more closely, noticing that unlike some of the other scrawny waifs in her care, Florence and Dulcie looked a decent size for their age. She wondered whether they had been stealing food from the dustbins again to look in such rude health.

"Shall we go now, Matron?" Dulcie wished she was anywhere but where they were and felt the sweat trickle down her back as she edged backwards towards the door.

Matron gripped Florence's arm again, prodding her muscles as though she was a prize cow at the market, before breaking into a sly smile. "It's high time you two went out into the world and made yourselves useful. Now that the cold weather has arrived, no doubt there will be plenty more unwanted wretches to take your place here and there are only so many mouths we can feed. Report to my office after breakfast tomorrow morning. I have the perfect person in mind who can put up with your shenanigans in return for a hard day's work."

"You mean we're being put out to work already?" Dulcie gulped nervously. "Will we come back here at night? This is the only place we know."

Matron gave her a pitying look. "Dear, dear, child. People in your position don't get to pick and choose. We've given you a wonderful start in life here at Chalsworth Orphanage...which I trust you are most grateful for. It's time for you to become a useful member of society now instead of being coddled under my care."

With one final painful pinch of their arms, she propelled them out of her office and slammed the door behind them. The quicker she was rid of them, the better, and her mind was made up. Even though she was meant to look after them until they were twelve years old, the employer she had in mind wouldn't ask difficult questions about their age, she was quite sure. Plus the extra coins he always slipped her would go nicely towards a more comfortable life for her old age.

"A night in the shed to make them behave better, and a new job to get them out of my sight...today's not so bad after all." Widow Ebworth straightened the picture of the saints that hung behind her desk and then poured herself a tot of gin. She gulped it down with a self-satisfied nod of appreciation at how well she ran the place.

* * *

"Don't make this any more difficult than it needs to be. Matron gave me my orders and you know I can't disobey them or there'll be hell to pay." Bernard Ellis pulled a ring of jangling keys from the depths of his coat pocket and selected the largest one. He unlocked the creaking wooden door and threw it open, grimacing as several rats scuttled away into the shadows of the old coal shed.

"Can't you just let us hide for the night, Bernard?" Florence gave him her best smile. "Matron's putting us out to work tomorrow I think, so it's our last night here anyway. We'll go behind the hay rack in the old stables and nobody need ever know. Please, Bernard, you know Dulcie is scared of the dark."

Bernard lowered his eyes guiltily and sighed. "I know, and I'm sorry. If it was down to me, I'd tell the constable and make sure she never punished any of you nippers this way again. 'Tis crueller than necessary in my mind. But if she found out I'd gone against her orders and let you off your punishment...my wife is expecting another baby again, you see. I can't afford to lose my job."

"Oh, I don't want to risk that. Never mind, we…we'll be fine."

Dulcie gripped Florence's hand tighter. "It's alright Florence. As long as you're with me, I won't find it so bad. And just think, if what Matron said is true, we'll never ever have to spend a night in the old coal shed again." She peered into the choking, cobweb-strewn darkness that lay beyond the door that Bernard was holding open for them and took a faltering step forward.

Bernard glanced over his shoulder and pulled some stale crusts from his pocket. "I managed to get these from the kitchen without anyone noticing. It ain't much but it might help keep your spirits up. Also, if you look in the corner you'll see that I've left an old blanket there. It's a bit moth-eaten but at least you'll be warmer than last time. I'll come and let you at first light, girls. Chin up."

Dulcie gave Bernard a shaky smile and pressed herself closer to Florence. The worst bit was always when Bernard closed the door. Seeing the last vestiges of light vanish and hearing the key turning in the lock was when Dulcie felt the panic starting to rise in her chest, making her gasp for breath.

Florence put her arm around Dulcie's shoulder and guided her to sit on the blanket, pulling it over their backs. "Which game shall we play? Our favourite food, or what we'd like for Christmas?"

Dulcie took a steadying breath and chuckled. "How about a new game? We could imagine what our new job will be like. I'll go first...I'm guessing that we'll be servants to Queen Victoria herself. We'll wear fur-lined capes when it's cold and we'll have the cosiest room together in the attic of a castle."

Florence shared the bread between them and munched thoughtfully, trying to ignore the cramping of hunger in her belly and the scuttling sound of the rats that had come out again, looking for crumbs. "I think we'll be working behind the stage at The Adelphi Theatre. Helping the performers get dressed, scooping up all the roses the audience throw at the end…"

As the snow fell softly outside, muffling the sounds of the town beyond the oppressive walls of the orphanage, Florence and Dulcie whispered their hopes and dreams for a better future, cuddling up close to stay warm. "I really don't mind what we do, as long as we work together," Dulcie said sleepily as she tightened the blanket around them. "Anything's better than being here, don't you think?"

Florence hugged her friend and started to hum a lullaby until she could tell from Dulcie's breathing that she had drifted off to sleep.

I wish…I wish we could both always be together and work for the kindest employer in the whole world. Florence stifled a yawn as her racing thoughts gradually slowed down. Maton had given so little away about where she was sending them that it was impossible to imagine where they might be in the next few days. Even though life at Chalsworth Orphanage was bleak, it was all that they had ever known and she didn't know whether to be excited or fearful of what might come next.

Dulcie whimpered in her sleep and Florence

wrapped her arms around her friend to banish the nightmares that always came when they had been punished this way. They huddled together in the claustrophobic, dank darkness of the shed until sleep finally carried Florence away to blissful oblivion until daybreak.

CHAPTER 2

❦

The carriage rumbled over the cobblestones of Chalsworth market square and Florence craned her neck for one last look at the orphanage as it receded into the distance. "Good riddance," she muttered under her breath, before nudging Dulcie with her elbow. "We won't miss that place, eh?"

She felt her spirits lift as they passed through the busy streets of the town. The honeyed stones of the town's buildings looked mellow against the pillowy mounds of snow that covered all the rooftops and in the distance, shouts of excitement pierced the air from the people who were skating on the frozen lake in the park.

Dulcie pulled her thin shawl tighter over her

shoulders against the sharp wind that blew up the valley. "I don't know why they didn't let us walk to Thruppley Mill, it's only on the outskirts of town, by all accounts. Look over there Florrie, the shops look so beautiful I could spend a whole day looking in the windows." Dulcie's cheeks were pink with excitement as her gaze darted from one delight to the next.

"Button it, you two." Mr Collier thumped the door of the carriage with his fist from where he was perched atop the box with the driver, bringing their excited chatter to an abrupt halt and making Dulcie shrink back. He leaned out and peered through the window at the mill's newest recruits. "Do you think we're going to risk a couple of runaways? You belong to the mill now, so the quicker we can get you started, the better," he said crisply.

"Charming," Florence whispered, with a wry smile. "I saw him slipping Matron a pouch of coins when we were leaving. No wonder she was so friendly to the fellow."

The girls leant back against the worn leather seat and watched the town roll past. The bowed windows of the shops were already adorned with Christmas decorations and the pavements bustled with elegant women clad in heavy velvet capes passing the time of day as their maids scurried forth to do the shopping.

"I'd give anything to be like them," Dulcie said with a wistful sigh. "Imagine being able to buy whatever food you liked, and having a jolly time in front of the roaring fire opening your presents. And with your own family there too. It would be like a miracle."

Florence's mouth watered as the smell of roasting chestnuts and coffee wafted from the braziers on the street corner.

"Penny a scoop!"

"Hot coffee and spiced buns!"

"One day, Dulcie. If we work hard, we both might meet two nice gentlemen and have families of our own." Florence grinned at her friend, letting her imagination run away with her. "I reckon Thruppley Mill might be the best thing that ever happens to us. We won't have to worry about Matron breathing down our necks, and we'll be earning a few coins each week too."

"Do you think it will be hard work though?" Dulcie whispered. "What if we don't do well enough and they send us back to the orphanage. I don't think I could bear it."

"We'll be fine, just follow my lead," Florence replied quietly. She was determined to put a brave face on things for Dulcie's sake, but inside, Florence could feel her nerves mounting. Going back to the orphanage wasn't an option so she was determined to make their new position at the mill a success.

Her thoughts drifted back to Matron's parting words to them both. By a strange twist of fate, Florence and Dulcie had both lost their mothers during childbirth. Her father had left her at the orphanage less than a month later, claiming he was joining the army, and Dulcie's father had died from typhoid, leaving her all alone.

"You'll never amount to anything," Matron had said waspishly from behind her desk. "Both of you were exceedingly unwanted children...and frankly, given your bad behaviour over the years, your fathers both had a lucky escape." She had signed the paperwork releasing them from her care with a flourish, before peering coldly over the top of her spectacles at them. "You're too high spirited, that's your problem. You need to learn your place and that's exactly why this job will be so good for you." She had crossed her arms and looked at them expectantly.

"Thank you, Matron," they had chorused, knowing what she was waiting for.

"Don't make me regret suggesting you to my friend Mr Collier," she had added. "He's a very important man at the mill so if you know what's good for you, you'll work hard and do as you're told. And if I find out Mr Collier isn't pleased with your work...well, make sure I don't." She had scowled at them one last time, before slamming the door shut once she was sure they were safely in Mr Collier's care.

"Look, that must be it." Dulcie jabbed Florence, breaking into her reverie. She leaned forward and used the corner of her shawl to rub the frost from the window and pointed towards a cluster of buildings. There were so many of them that it looked almost like a village in its own right. "It...it doesn't look so different from the orphanage," she added quietly. "There's a big wall all the way around."

Sure enough, a few moments later the driver turned the horses off the road, through an imposing set of iron gates, under a large sign announcing it to be Thruppley Mill. The carriage came to a halt and Mr Collier jumped down, beckoning them out.

"Follow me," he said curtly.

The two girls clutched their small bundle of belongings and scurried after him, slithering through the snow of the yard, then up the steps into a large office.

"Add their details to our records please, Mr Samuel, and send them to their dormitory with the usual instructions."

The clerk dipped the nib of his pen into the inkwell and scratched their names into a vast ledger, frowning with concentration in the gloomy corner of the office where his desk resided. A feeble light guttered in the lamp behind him and his cheeks were tinged with purple above the woollen scarf that was wound tightly around his neck.

"Good morning, Sir," Dulcie whispered. A draught trickled around their ankles from the ill-fitting windows and Dulcie's teeth chattered as they stood waiting for their instructions.

"It's very cold for you in here Mr Samuel," Florence said. She gave him an engaging smile, determined to make a good first impression.

"No point wasting good coal when I can put another coat on, child. Mr DeVere encourages us to be frugal; says it's for the good of the mill so we can employ more people." The clerk sneezed into a voluminous handkerchief before folding his hands around a steaming cup of coffee. He looked at them more closely taking in their ragged dresses and gaping shoes. "You won't need to worry about being cold here at Thruppley," he added with a mirthless chuckle. "You'll be too busy to notice it in the weaving room, and too tired at night for it to bother you."

Dulcie darted Florence a nervous look. "Do we get fed a nice hot dinner every day, Mr Samuel? We haven't eaten since yesterday morning, you see." She gazed longingly at the wedge of fruitcake that was next to his coffee cup.

"My, my...you're very forward you two. Mrs Ebworth usually supplies us with nice quiet children. I hope you won't make any trouble. The manager, Mr Collier doesn't like troublemakers, especially when we're due an inspection by Mr DeVere. He's the owner of the mill," he added. "You'll soon learn who everyone is."

"Sorry Mr Samuel. You won't hear a peep out of us again," Florence said hastily.

He looked at them through narrowed eyes, then let a wheeze of laughter. "It's not me you need to worry about, child. I'm just a lowly clerk. But you don't want to get on the wrong side of Mr Collier." He lowered his voice and looked to check that the door was closed. "Between you and me, he can be a bit short-tempered, if you get my drift."

Florence nodded and grinned back at him. "Thank you for helping us settle in."

"Think nothing of it. You need to go back down the steps and across the yard to the furthest dormitory...you'll see there's a big oak tree next to it. Find two empty beds and put your belongings away, then go through the large blue door into the weaving room, as quickly as you can."

Dulcie and Florence bobbed a curtsey and turned to leave.

"To answer your question, Miss Pickering, as long as you behave, you do have a hot meal every day. Your first one will be at six o'clock sharp tonight when the bell sounds." He smiled at the look of relief on Dulcie's face.

"Oh, thank you, Sir, anything's got to be better than the orphanage food." Dulcie's stomach rumbled as if to underline her point.

"And one last thing..." Mr Samuel rifled through the papers on his desk already moving on to this next task. "We have a lot of rules here at Thruppley Mill. You'll learn them soon enough.

But the most important one is that when the owners visit, you must be on your very best behaviour. Seen and not heard. Is that understood?"

Florence nodded and they scurried away. "We'll be sure to do exactly as we're told," she called back over her shoulder. "We're just happy to have left the orphanage Mr Samuel and we're going to be the best little workers you have here, just you wait and see."

Ten minutes later, Florence smoothed her apron down and took a deep breath before heaving the large blue door of the weaving room open. "Ready Dulcie? This is our chance to put Matron and all her horrible punishments behind us and have a new start."

Dulcie giggled nervously as they crept into the cavernous interior. "I hope they let us work next to each other," she replied, but her words were lost in the thundering roar of the machines that greeted them.

The rest of the day passed in a blur. No sooner had the two girls scurried to the desk at the front of the room than they were marched off in separate directions to get to work. Row upon row of looms stood as far as they could see and the air was thick with dust that made their eyes water and caught at the back of their throats with every breath.

"Stand here and do exactly what I do." The dark-haired woman who had steered Florence to a huge loom cupped her hands around Florence's ear to make herself heard.

Florence had nodded, fumbling with the bobbins to start with, but gradually finding the rhythm of the repetitive task of keeping them fed with fresh wool so the machine never ran out.

There was so much happening in the weaving room that Florence hardly knew which direction to look. To her untrained eye, it seemed as though there were a million threads feeding into the machine, like a spider's web. Pistons plunged and valves hissed with steam. The constant clattering noise of it all pulsed through her eardrums, driving everything from her mind other than keeping up with the unrelenting march of the weaving shuttles and twisting bobbins of wool in every colour imaginable. Unable to speak over the noise, she followed the woman as she pointed out each stage of the process that turned the myriad of threads into a smooth sheet of woven worsted broadcloth. By the time the bell rang at the end of

THE MAID'S WINTER WISH

the day and the machines fell mercifully silent at the end of their shift, Florence's eyes were burning from the dust and her body ached with tiredness from the unfamiliar work.

* * *

"DON'T DAWDLE, else we'll miss all the best grub." A thin woman grabbed Florence and Dulcie's arms pushing them in line ahead of her as they filed across the snowy yard under Mr Collier's watchful eye. She gave them a kindly smile. "Collier's asked me to help you settle in," she added by way of explanation.

"Thank you...it's all a bit overwhelming," Florence replied. "What's your name?"

"Helen Crindle," the woman answered. "You must be Florence, eh? Mr Collier told me the one with dark hair was called Florence and the one with blonde hair is Dulcie. I wondered if you were sisters, but I can see you don't look much alike."

Dulcie nodded, finally finding her voice. "We were both abandoned at the orphanage as babies, ten years ago. And you're right, we aren't sisters, but I wish we were. We love each other as much as any sisters would." She linked arms with Florence, suddenly feeling shy as they entered the dining room and dozens of faces turned to stare at them.

"You'll find it's not so very different from the orphanage, I expect," Helen said with a roll of her eyes. "Rules for everything, bells to wake us, and don't make any mistakes, or else. We collect our food and sit at these long tables. And if you're late, there's nothing until the morning, so look lively."

"The food is definitely better than what we had at the orphanage." Florence mopped up the last drops of her oxtail stew with a crust of bread and licked every crumb from her fingers, savouring the final mouthful of their meal. After the incessant roaring noise of the weaving room, the quiet murmur of chatter at the tables felt like a welcome relief.

Dulcie's cheeks had regained some colour and she eked out the remains of her mug of tea. "How long have you been here?" she asked their new friend curiously.

"Too long," Helen chuckled. "I came when I was twelve years old and I'm eighteen now...my Ma got sick and couldn't afford to feed the little 'uns after my scoundrel of a father got thrown in jail, so I was sent here to work. It's not so bad," she added. "We get a roof over our heads and a hot meal every day. And on Sundays, we're allowed a couple of hours off after church to do our laundry and clean the dormitory. Sometimes we're even allowed to go home, for those of us with families near enough to visit."

Dulcie gulped down the last of her tea. "And will we be here forever, do you think?"

"If it was up to Mr Collier and Mr DeVere, we'd be here until we're carried out feet first in a box." Helen's eyes clouded even though she tried to maintain her good cheer so as not to frighten her new charges.

"That sounds awful. You mean people actually die working here?" Dulcie's eyes rounded in horror.

"She's exaggerating, I'm sure."

Helen shrugged. "There's plenty of illness and the work takes it out of you until you get used to it. We like to joke that the only way out for a woman is getting married or being too exhausted to work anymore." She rubbed the callouses on her bony hands. "Trouble is, there aren't many men would look twice at someone like me," she added, and the corners of her mouth drooped with regret. "I was always a sickly child and the doctor told Ma I'd likely never have children of my own."

Florence patted Helen's hand. "Well we haven't got any family, but we don't let it get us down, do we, Dulcie. Now that you're looking out for us, it could be like we're your family."

Helen chuckled at Florence's comment. "Mr Collier told me you two were very forward with your comments. Well, actually he said you needed to learn some manners, but I like you...we'll get along just fine, I can tell. Now finish up and I'll take you to your dormitory. We're in the same one. We have one hour to read and do mending and other jobs, then it's bedtime."

Later that night, Florence pulled the thin blanket up to her chin and wriggled to get comfortable on the lumpy mattress beneath her. Their narrow iron beds were at the furthest end of the dormitory and the meagre heat from the stove did little to keep the chill at bay. She peered up at the high windows. The moonlight was like a silver wash against the glitter of ice that coated the glass and her body convulsed with a shiver that was as much about fearing for their futures as the bone-chilling cold that gripped her.

What if this is as good as our lives will ever be. Rising before dawn and working until our fingers bleed every day. The bleak thought slid into Florence's mind before she could stop it and she sighed, tugging the blanket higher to block out the sound of someone softly crying from further down the line of beds. She thought about what Matron had said about her and Dulcie never amounting to anything and folded her arms tightly around herself. She would prove her wrong. If it was the last thing she did...she would figure out a way to try and give herself and Dulcie a better life than the scraps of existence that Matron believed they were worth.

CHAPTER 3

*F*lorence dragged the brush through her long chestnut hair and deftly braided it into a tidy plait. She licked her fingers to smooth back the curls that always defied the brush and sprang back to frame her face, but as per usual, they refused to stay where she wanted them to.

"Hurry up, or they'll leave without us." Dulcie nudged Florence out of the way to look at her own reflection in the one fly-spotted mirror in their dormitory. "You look as pretty as ever, and I look like I've been dragged through a hedge backwards," she muttered, jabbing some extra hairpins into her bun to keep it in place.

Florence leant in closer and blew her a kiss in the mirror. "Don't be silly, Dulcie. You know the boys always look at you when we're walking to church. Not that we want that sort of attention," she added with a giggle. "I swear we'll both still be here, working our fingers to the bone at Thruppley Mill until we're decrepit old spinsters if Mr Collier has anything to do with it."

"Don't get me started," Helen chimed in. "Fred Larson handed me a cup of tea after church the other day and Mr Collier gave me a proper telling off the next morning. He said Miss Peabody had informed him that I was making eyes at Fred across the aisle during the vicar's sermon and if I didn't watch out I'd be labelled a fallen woman by the whole parish." She rolled her eyes and sighed.

"One day, Helen. You'll meet a good man and Collier won't be able to do a thing about it." Florence shot her a sympathetic look.

"Chance would be a fine thing," Helen replied, shaking her head. "We've been friends for a while now, ain't we...I mean it's two and a half years since you came to work at the mill...but have you ever seen me walking out with a sweetheart?"

Florence shrugged. "You're only twenty, there's plenty of time yet. Maybe someone will take a shine to you at the Fayre today or you might bump into Fred." She rummaged in her dress pocket and pulled out the burgundy velvet hair ribbon she had been saving for best, to tie the end of her plait. It was her most treasured possession; a gift from the mill owners the previous Christmas, when every member of staff had received a small token in appreciation of their work during the year.

"Here, this colour will look perfect for you." She held the ribbon up against Helen's mousy brown hair and nodded decisively, feeling a glow of satisfaction as her friend's face lit up with pleasure. Helen might have already resigned herself to being left on the shelf, but Florence knew that she was one of the kindest people at the mill and one day she would make a nice young man a wonderful wife. If losing out on wearing the ribbon herself helped Helen's cause, it was a small price to pay, she told herself.

"I can't believe we're being allowed a whole afternoon out," Dulcie exclaimed for the third time in as many hours.

"It's no thanks to Mr Collier," Helen replied as she wrapped her summer shawl around her shoulders. "I overheard him complaining to Mr Samuel that Mrs DeVere's meddling would be the downfall of the mill if they weren't careful. Apparently, it was Mrs DeVere who persuaded her husband that a day out for all of us would be good for morale and that it was an opportunity to show everyone that the DeVere family are generous employers."

"Generous? Well I'm not sure I'd go that far, but I for one am delighted she meddled," Florence said happily. "We've never been to anything like the Chalsworth Summer Fayre before."

"Do you remember that Matron always said there were far too many chances for us to misbehave on this sort of day out," Dulcie reminisced.

An hour later, Florence and Dulcie stood in the warm summer sunshine, drinking in the scene in front of them. Chalsworth Summer Fayre was an annual event, held on the common at the edge of town and the gaily coloured posters announcing it had been nailed to trees around the district for weeks.

"Look at all the animals. Do you think it's safe?" Dulcie jumped back as the drovers herded their best sheep and cattle into the ring where they would be judged by the town's mayor. A thickset Hereford bull bellowed, turning his head to stare at Dulcie and she darted behind Florence with a shriek, before the farmer tweaked the rope on his nose ring and he lumbered on past them with a swish of his tail.

Florence lifted her hand to shade her eyes. There was so much to see, she didn't know where to start. "Let's walk around the stalls first, and then we can see which animals won the prizes. I'm sure we'll be fine as long as we don't get in anyone's way."

They linked arms and strolled towards the gaily coloured stalls that were lined up against the hedge. Hawkers plucked at their sleeves beckoning for them to come and buy.

"Jack-in-the-box! See how he jumps."

"Three shies a penny!"

"A twist o' humbugs! Turkish delight! Get'yer toffee 'ere!"

The crowds surged around Florence and Dulcie and the air was filled with the competing shouts of the stall-holders selling their wares. Gaggles of children darted between everybody like shoals of fish before returning to their parents and Florence felt a sudden pang of regret that she and Dulcie had been denied such simple pleasures when they were younger.

Further along the field, the stalls of ginger-bread, pickled whelks, and penny toys gave way to the more exotic travelling performers. Dogs dancing in frilly costumes and jumping through hoops. A ponderous elephant, trumpeting so loudly it made the onlookers scream with fright. Bearded ladies and jugglers walked amongst them, holding their hands out for money, and the girls giggled as they watched three clowns doing a tumbling routine that involved teasing a wealthy gentleman they had selected from the crowd.

"My sides hurt from laughing so much." Florence and Dulcie paused for a moment under the shade of a large oak tree. They shared the bag of crumbly buttery fudge Florence had purchased, enjoying the rare sweet treat as it melted in their mouths. "Shall we go and watch the brass band for a while?"

"I think I might sit here for a while," Dulcie said, fanning herself. "I wasn't expecting it to be this warm. You go on and I'll catch you up in a bit."

Florence gave her a grin and hurried away. Her senses were reeling from all the noise and bright colours and delicious smells. After the everyday monotony of work in the mill, she didn't want to miss a single thing, not to mention she still had a couple of pennies in her pocket to spend on what-ever took her fancy.

As she got closer to the makeshift bandstand

that had been assembled for the day, she felt her spirits lift. There wasn't a cloud in the sky and it was a perfect summer's day. A crowd had gathered and the conductor turned around to address the audience.

"As it's the centenary year of the Chalsworth Summer Fayre, we will be performing a medley of your favourite tunes." He smiled as the onlookers gave a round of applause. "Also..." He winked at the children who were standing at the front. "We'll be taking suggestions. If you'd like to hear a special tune, speak to my dear wife over there, and we'll choose one to play at the end."

"Oh how delightful, Ernest." The woman standing in front of Florence clapped her hands together and linked arms with her beau.

The conductor gave everyone a bow, then turned back to face the band. He tapped his baton on the podium that held his sheet music before nodding and starting to conduct the first tune. The air filled with a lively waltz and within moments the young children at the front of the crowd were arm in arm, gliding over the grass with giggles of delight while their parents watched with indulgent smiles.

The jolly music had soon gathered a bigger

crowd and Florence realised with a start that Mr Collier was hovering at the edge of the gathering, accompanied by a drab looking woman who Florence assumed must be his wife. He stood with folded arms, looking as though it was the last place he wanted to be, frowning with irritation every time he caught sight of one of the mill workers.

"Lawks, he can't even be happy for us to enjoy one measly afternoon out all year," Florence muttered to herself. She edged backwards, not wanting him to spot her. His looming presence had taken the shine off the performance and she decided to go and find Dulcie again.

Suddenly, out of the corner of her eye, Florence saw a boy who seemed to be watching her. He wore a loose coat over his shirt and had a spotted handkerchief tied at his neck that gave him a rakish air. She felt herself flush, not used to such attention. It was usually Dulcie, with her golden hair and bright blue eyes, who attracted admiring stares from the gawking local boys who nudged one another with fumbled attempts at conversation. She lifted her chin and tried to ignore him, tapping her foot nonchalantly in time with the popular music hall tune that the band was now playing.

A moment later, she saw the boy threading his way between the crowd. She looked more closely. Every so often he paused, scanning the crowd of onlookers instead of watching the band. She noticed that as he strolled casually between everyone, he seemed to favour stopping next to the couples who were well dressed. With a shiver of understanding, she realised that he was a dipper. His touch was so fast that it was only by staring hard at him that she saw the stealthy reach of his hand into his targets' coat pockets, in and out, done in a flash, before he wandered on.

Florence craned her neck, looking to see if there was a constable nearby. In the distance, she saw a bobby chatting to the vicar and she grappled with her conscience. Should she report the boy?

She peered into the crowd again and realised that he was standing directly behind Mr Collier. He brushed against him, then hurried away, but not before he had turned to look directly at Florence, giving her a sly wink.

"You can't do that…" Florence's words came out as a whisper, but before she could raise the alarm, she had a moment of clarity. It wouldn't bode well for her to get involved. Mr Collier would find a way to hold her responsible, even though it was nothing to do with her, she was sure.

"I've been robbed!"

"Oi, someone's had my pocket watch!"

Shouts suddenly erupted up from the wealthier folk as they realised what had happened and the constable came running over.

"Did anyone see who did this?" The constable pushed between the crowds, demanding answers.

"No Sir, we didn't see nothing."

"It wasn't me, I promise."

Children scuttled away, not wanting to be dragged into the situation and Florence caught sight of Mr Collier's thunderous expression as he patted his pockets, realising that he too had been robbed. His wife tried to soothe him, stroking his arm, but he threw her off and stomped away, cursing loudly that the Fayre was a magnet for thieves and drunkards and they never should have come.

After the initial commotion had died down, Florence decided she could go and find Dulcie again without it looking as though she was running away. She hurried across the common, taking the longer route to avoid bumping into Mr Collier.

"Lookout miss!" A wagon rumbled towards Florence, bumping over the uneven ground, going faster than it should have been. "You need to pay attention instead of daydreaming." The driver scowled and tugged on the reins but the horse was prancing in its harness, kicking out at a wasp that buzzed under its belly. "Slow down, you stupid animal." The driver stood up in his seat and yanked harder at the reins, but it was futile and the mound of logs stacked up on his wagon started to rock dangerously.

A sound like a rifle shot split the air and the rope holding the logs in place suddenly snapped. Florence stumbled backwards but her foot caught on a tussock of grass. It was too late. The logs were cascading from the wagon, rolling in her direction faster than she could move and she felt herself falling, knowing that she would be crushed before she had the chance to get out of the way.

"Easy there. You'll be alright." The voice came from far away, and Florence shook her head slightly, wondering if she was dreaming. She could feel the warm sun on her face and she smiled.

"Can you sit up?" The voice sounded more insistent this time, and Florence frowned, opening her eyes slowly. She looked up, expecting to see the blue sky. A face swam into view. Freckles. Hazel coloured eyes that were flecked with green. Tousled sandy coloured hair...and a spotted handkerchief."

"It's you!" Florence gasped and sat up quickly, almost bumping heads with the boy who had been leaning over, staring at her with a worried expression. "I haven't got anything worth stealing so don't even think about it," she muttered, scrambling to her feet.

"Nice to meet you too," the boy said with a wry chuckle. He folded his arms and looked her up and down, before tilting his head towards the wagon driver who was reloading his wagon nearby. "You didn't get hit by a log, but I reckon you had a bit of a bump to your head when you fell over your own feet. Are you always that clumsy?"

Florence bristled. "What makes you think I shouldn't report you to the constable? I saw exactly what you were doing. You were lucky you didn't get caught." She looked more closely at the boy and her heart skipped a beat as he grinned back at her, apparently without a care in the world.

"If you were going to report me, you would have done it already," he said nonchalantly. "Besides, I know what a rotter that Mr Collier is to all you poor souls who work at the mill. Why do you think I robbed him?"

"How do you know about him?" Florence asked slowly, her curiosity piqued. The boy was right though. She had to admit that it had given her an unexpected feeling of pleasure to see Mr Collier on the receiving end of the misfortune he was usually so quick to dispense to others.

"Everyone around these parts knows what he's like," the boy replied. "Anyway, I can't loiter. I've done my good deed for the day, so I reckon we're even, don't you?" He turned to leave.

"Wait. I haven't had a chance to say thank you." Florence straightened her rumpled dress and smoothed her hair back."

"You missed a bit," the boy said. He stepped closer and plucked a leaf from her plait, dropping it in her hand with a grin.

Florence looked up into his face and felt the strange flutter in her chest again, almost as though she couldn't catch her breath. "What's your name? Do you live in Chalsworth?"

"Hunter...that's what they call me. But don't tell anyone, eh?" He tapped the side of his nose.

"I'm Florence. I'm still not sure whether I should be thanking you or reporting you to the bobbies, but...don't get caught, alright? Or how about doing a proper day's work like the rest of us. You'll end up in the clink if you're not careful." She felt exasperated as Hunter lifted his hands in a carefree shrug and grinned again.

"This is all I know," he replied. "Anyway, I'd better get off, else Pa will have my guts for garters." He tightened his coat and strolled away, leaving Florence staring after him.

Suddenly he turned around and walked back towards her. "Don't let Mr Collier boss you around too much Florence. You seem like a good sort, and bullies like him shouldn't be allowed to make people's lives a misery. It ain't right." With that, he reached out and squeezed her hand. "Until next time, Florence." He strode away, giving her another wink over his shoulder, before joining the stream of people who were strolling home and within seconds he had vanished from her sight.

You're a strange sort of boy...a thief. By rights I should dislike you...but you seemed like someone I'd like to have as a friend. Confusing thoughts and emotions filled Florence's mind as she replayed the encounter between Hunter and herself.

"Where have you been? I've been looking everywhere for you. Did you hear there've been lots of robberies? Apparently, there was a vicious gang of thieves and people feared for their lives." Dulcie's urgent words pulled Florence from her thoughts as she hurried breathlessly towards her. "I nodded off under the tree and missed all the excitement which is just typical."

"Oh, yes...I heard something had happened," Florence murmured. She looked past Dulcie, but Hunter was nowhere to be seen.

"Are you alright?" Dulcie tugged at Florence's arm. "You seem a bit distracted."

Florence focused on her friend and smiled. "It was the strangest thing. I fell over and this boy called Hunter came to my rescue."

Dulcie's eyes rounded with intrigue and she looked around. "A boy? Where is he?"

"He's gone. It was all over in a matter of minutes. Let's go and have another walk around the stalls, we've still got a bit of time before we have to leave." Another wagon rumbled past and Florence hastily moved out of the way. The wheels sent up a cloud of dust and she sneezed loudly. As she went to pull her handkerchief from her dress pocket, her fingers felt something metallic instead of the cotton she had expected. She pulled the object out and found a shiny button between her fingers. It was embossed with a delicate rose that glinted in the sun.

"Where did you get that from, it's so pretty." Dulcie sounded slightly envious, even though they both knew it wasn't worth much.

Florence looked at the button again, with puzzlement, and then burst out laughing. "That boy...I reckon he must have slipped it into my pocket, the cheeky so and so."

"Maybe he wanted you to have something to remember him by," Dulcie said with a grin. "What a grand adventure….this is the best day we've had for a long time."

CHAPTER 4

$\mathcal{M}$r Collier stamped the snow from his feet and loosened the woollen scarf around his neck. Although it was only the end of November, winter had come early to Chalsworth and the surrounding district. The icy wind blasted through the door behind him, and he closed it firmly before the workers started complaining about being cold.

He climbed the steps to the small platform at the front of the dining room and cast a withering look over the workers who had gathered in front of him. He cleared his throat and searched the pinched faces, looking for one in particular. "Mr and Mrs DeVere are coming to do an inspection of the mill later today, as you know. But it has been brought to my attention that something has been taking place which is against the rules."

A ripple of whispers ran through the workers as they lowered their eyes, not wanting to incur the wrath of the bully who seemed to delight in making their lives even harder than they already were.

Dulcie darted a worried look towards Florence who was whispering to one of the younger children, telling them not to be afraid.

"Florence May, please step forward."

Florence jumped upon hearing her name and the people around her shuffled back slightly, leaving her standing alone under Mr Collier's stern gaze.

"I...I'm here, Sir." Florence lifted her chin, knowing what was coming. She returned Dulcie's look with the hint of a smile to let her know that she would be alright.

Mr Collier paused, feeling irritated that Florence didn't have that glimmer of fear in her eyes which most people did when he picked on them. His face darkened as he ruminated on the fact that in his opinion, she had been nothing but a thorn in his side in the six years since he collected her from the orphanage. He had told Matron

Ebworth on numerous occasions since, and now she was more careful to only send the most obedient children his way.

He drew himself up to his full height and a hush fell over the room. "This wretched girl has been stealing." Collier's face flushed with anger and he raised his hand to point to her. "Florence May has decided that instead of knowing her place and doing as she's told...she would help herself to extra food from the kitchens when the cook's back was turned."

"I only did it because—"

"Silence!" Mr Collier bellowed, cutting over her words. "I do not want your paltry excuses and explanations. You've been warned about breaking the rules before, you insolent specimen. As soon as Mr DeVere's visit is over I will be giving you the appropriate punishment. And until then, I suggest you stay out of my sight and behave impeccably, otherwise...otherwise, I'll take the strap to you so hard you'll wish you'd never come to Thruppley Mill." The spittle flew from his mouth and he thumped his fist on the table, sending a tray of cups smashing to the ground.

"Yes Sir, of course, Sir." Florence bobbed her head and held her trembling hands demurely by her side, trying not to let her dismay show. She could feel the hard outline of the button she always kept in her dress pocket and it gave her courage. She had never told anyone that she secretly thought of as her lucky button, ever since that day at the Fayre a few years ago and a faint image of Hunter...the boy who had been so full of life and laughter floated into her mind again. She wondered briefly where he was now and whether he had ended up in jail as she'd warned against.

"Now smarten yourselves up and remember, Mr DeVere pays your wages and very generously allows you to live like kings under his patronage here at Thruppley Mill, with the help of my trusted management. So I expect him to be delighted with everything that he sees today, do you understand?"

Dozens of heads nodded hastily in agreement and he scowled at them again before marching briskly back to his office. "Give me strength...that Florence is nothing but trouble and she needs to learn her lesson once and for all," he muttered.

As soon as he was back in his office he took a fortifying swig of brandy from the bottle he kept tucked at the back of his drawer. The warmth spread through his chest and he looked at his reflection in the glass-fronted bookcase, twirling the ends of his moustache and straightening his collar in readiness for Mr DeVere's visit. He was fast losing patience with the lackadaisical habits of the mill workers under his management, and the way they constantly pestered him with their seemingly never-ending illnesses and accidents. He had told his wife only last week that he had never had the misfortune to work with such a clumsy, unhealthy bunch and if he didn't get his annual pay rise due to their ineptitude there would be merry hell to pay.

"Collier's got it in for you now, Florence. Is it true what he said?" Helen briskly swept up the broken shards of crockery and shook her head.

"Well...yes I suppose so." Florence shrugged. Those two little nippers who joined from the orphanage last week didn't finish their work on time and missed out on their dinner, poor things. So I popped into the kitchen after lights out and got an old loaf of bread that was probably going to be fed to the pigs the next day anyway."

Dulcie's eyes rounded at Florence's bold admission. "Lawks, Florence, what on earth did you do that for? You know he's already angry with you for suggesting that if we could have an extra break for a cup of tea it might help us work more efficiently."

"Remember those terrible nights in the coal shed, Dulcie? When we were so hungry it felt like we might faint clean away." Florence patted Dulcie's arm, seeing that she had gone pale, thinking back to Matron's punishments. "That's why I did it," she added. "Nobody should have to go to bed hungry, least of all those little mites who are still learning how everything works at the mill and can hardly stand up at the end of the day because they're so exhausted. It's just not fair on them."

"I suppose you're right," Dulcie conceded. "We were lucky to have Helen looking out for us when we started out here all those years ago. I'm sure I would have gone hungry without you being our guardian angel." She grinned at Helen, knowing that her quick thinking had saved their bacon from Mr Collier's punishments on more than one occasion.

"Ha! I'd hardly call myself that," Helen chuckled. "Mr Collier seems to be getting worse than ever, though. Nothing seems to please him, no matter how hard we work. It's the pressure from all the competing mills up North, I reckon. One of the fellows in the packing room told me that Mr DeVere told Collier he has to keep the machines running more hours in the day to stay ahead of them, otherwise we all might lose our jobs."

"It never did take much to make Collier cross, but he does seem to have taken a particular dislike to me over the years." Florence stacked a pile of dirty plates onto a tray and carried them towards the kitchen. "I'll just have to take my punishment," she added. "And I'd do it all over again because I can't bear to see the younger ones suffering. I'll just have to make sure I don't get caught next time," she added, with a defiant grin.

"Honestly, I don't know how she's so uncon- cerned," Dulcie muttered to Helen. "I still quake in my boots every time Mr Collier looks in my direc- tion. You'd think I'd have got used to it after all this time." She stifled a yawn and closed her eyes for a moment, thinking longingly of her narrow bed. They had been working an extra three hours a day in the week running up to the inspection and she felt dead on her feet.

"Come along, sleepy head." Florence smiled as she grabbed Dulcie's arm to hurry across the yard to the weaving room. "All we have to do is get through today without making any mistakes and hopefully Mr Grumpy Collier will be happier and let us stop work a bit earlier, seeing as it's only a few weeks until Christmas."

The next few hours passed in the usual whirl of activity amidst the roar of the machines. Florence's saving grace was that she was a quick worker, deftly keeping the bobbins free from the tangles that could halt the machine. Helen had told her in no uncertain terms that every minute that was wasted with a machine standing idle would cost the mill dearly in lost production. Florence had learned the hard way that this was the worst thing to send Mr Collier into a rage.

She eyed the clock on the wall, noting that it was nearly time for them to stop for a drink of water. Suddenly there was a flurry of commotion at the far end of the weaving room and Mr Collier swept in with Mr DeVere by his side. The owner of the mill cut an imposing figure. He was tall with greying hair that swept back from a high forehead and his brown eyes darted back and forth, missing nothing.

She could see Mr Collier pausing to admonish one of the young boys who had missed a speck of dust on the floor, clipping him around the ear when Mr DeVere's attention was elsewhere.

She stood on tiptoes, wondering whether Mr DeVere would come as far as the loom where she worked. Suddenly she noticed that Dulcie had slumped over her machine. She had complained about feeling exhausted earlier that day and Florence felt a rush of terror as she realised that Dulcie had fallen asleep at her station.

"Wake up, Dulcie," Florence shouted, but the words were drowned out by the clattering of the loom. Florence waved her hands frantically, making Helen glare at her.

As if in slow motion, Florence saw Dulcie's head nod forwards. To her horror, she saw that the boy standing next to her was too busy looking at Mr Collier to notice Dulcie was in danger.

"Save her!" She screamed as she saw Dulcie's arm being snatched into the jaws of the loom. "Out of my way." Florence barged past the children in her way, sprinting towards her friend. She yanked her roughly back, seconds before the piston began its descent, just in the nick of time to save her arm from being crushed to a pulp. Scarlet blood splattered down the front of Dulcie's apron and her eyes rounded with horror as her legs gave way and she collapsed into Florence's arms.

Before Florence had a chance to cry for

assistance, Mr Collier had grasped them both firmly as one of the other workers distracted Mr DeVere and propelled them through the nearest door into the corridor.

"Are you determined to ruin this visit?" A vein throbbed in Mr Collier's forehead and his eyes glinted with anger. "Sort yourself out, girl." He shook Dulcie, as her eyes fluttered open again.

"It was an accident, Sir," Florence interjected. "It's nothing too serious, but she was lucky she didn't lose her arm."

"I...I'm ever so sorry, Mr Collier. I don't know what came over me." Dulcie glanced down at her hand which was still dripping blood and paled again, leaning against Florence for comfort.

Collier paced backwards and forwards, thinking about what to do next. "Take her to the washroom and get her cleaned up. Then go to the office to get Mr Samuel to write a report, then go back to your dormitory, both of you. Hopefully, Mr DeVere didn't notice and the day can continue as planned." He looked at Florence through narrowed eyes. "Don't think this little event will get you out of your punishment either. If anything I'm even crosser with you, Florence. Every time something happens to disrupt my day, you seem to be at the heart of it. You'll still be getting a much-deserved beating, just as soon as Mr DeVere has left."

Florence nodded, knowing that it was futile to appeal to his better nature. She tightened her grip around Dulcie, lifting her up carefully as Mr Collier hurried away. "Come on, you'll be alright once we get a bandage on you. I'll ask Cook if you can have a cup of hot, sweet tea for the shock."

Dulcie gave her a weak smile before bursting into tears. "I didn't mean to get you into more trouble Florence. I've been so tired, and then I came over a bit strange, what with trying to have everything perfect for the visit. I must have just nodded off."

"Hush now, it could have been a lot worse," Florence said, mopping Dulcie's tears away with her handkerchief. "Maybe you're coming down with a cold, or more likely you're exhausted. Collier behaves as though we're machines, like those wretched looms of his."

Ten minutes later, Dulcie's hand was clean and wrapped in a strip of cloth from the bottom of Florence's apron until she could get it bandaged properly. "I'd better go to the office and let Mr Samuel know what's happened, like Mr Collier said. You wait here and then I'll take you to the dormitory. You might still feel a bit wobbly." She helped Dulcie to a nearby chair and set off for the clerk's office at a brisk trot.

The door creaked as she let herself in and Florence was surprised to see an elegantly dressed woman standing with her back to her. Mr Samuel was nowhere to be seen and Florence crept forwards, not knowing whether to announce her presence or not.

The woman sighed as she gazed out at the snowy hills beyond the mill. "My darling boy...how can I bear another year passing without you..." Her voice was barely more than a whisper. "I wish...I wish I'd never gone out that night and taken my eyes off you..." Her shoulders drooped and her head bowed as a sob escaped from her.

"Are you alright ma'am?" Florence could hear the heart-wrenching pain in the woman's tears and without thinking, she stepped forwards and put her arm around her to comfort her.

"Oh...oh, I thought I was alone." The woman dashed the tears from her eyes, looking embarrassed.

"I'm sorry ma'am, I didn't mean to listen to what you were saying. You just sounded so sad...and not long before Christmas too. Is there anything I can do to help? Shall I fetch a cup of tea? Here, why don't you sit down." Florence pulled Mr Samuel's chair from behind the desk and helped the woman into it.

"It's this time of year, you see. This is when I lost my boy, all those years ago. I keep hoping the pain will ease, but seeing the snow and other people feeling so jolly...all it does is remind me of what I've lost."

Florence nodded and passed her a glass of water. "Christmas used to make me sad too, ma'am. What with having no family of my own. But I'm lucky to have Dulcie, who's my best friend in all the world. She's an orphan as well, and when I do my best to cheer her up...it's strange, but it makes me feel happier too. Maybe you could try something like that. It does help, I promise."

The woman dabbed her cheeks again and returned the lace handkerchief to her reticule, looking more closely at Florence. "That sounds very wise for someone so young. What's your name, child?"

"I'm Florence May, ma'am. And I'm not that young. I just turned sixteen years old."

"Well the manager must be very pleased to have such a perceptive girl working here."

"I don't know about that, ma'am." Florence gave a rueful shrug. "Mr Collier's got it in for me at the moment, for not letting the little 'uns go hungry, but I reckon he likes me really because I'm a good little worker. It'll blow over soon enough," she added with a grin.

"Hmm, Mr Collier does rule the place with a rod of iron, I've heard." The woman gave Florence a thoughtful look. "You know, I've just lost one of my best maids...she's about your age...I wonder..."

Florence felt her pulse starting to quicken. "Dulcie and I would make the best sort of maids, ma'am. We're quick to learn and we work ever so hard."

"Oh, I was really only thinking of one position," the woman replied hastily. "I'm not sure we could justify taking on two new maids."

Florence's face fell. "I can't leave my friend behind ma'am, I'm sorry. She's like a sister to me. We're the same age, you see. Even though we look nothing alike, I think of her as being like my twin and when we left the orphanage to come and work here, we promised each other we'd never be parted."

"Like twins? That's such a precious thing to say, and more meaningful to me than you'll ever know." The woman gulped and her eyes misted over again. "In that case, my mind is made up. I shall tell my husband you're both coming to work for me. You shall be a maid for us, and I'll decide what your friend Dulcie can do all in good time."

"Honestly, ma'am? You really mean it?" Florence hopped up and down, not knowing whether to curtsey, laugh, or cry with delight.

The woman chuckled at her excitement and her smile lit up her face like the sun coming out from behind a cloud. "What a curious encounter, today of all days." She shook her head and stood up, touching Florence lightly on her shoulder. "I haven't even introduced myself, where are my manners? I'm Evelyn DeVere. My husband, Robert DeVere owns Thruppley Mill. You and Dulcie will come and live at our home, Bisley Court, which is just along the valley from here. We'll make the arrangements as soon as Mr Samuel gets back."

Florence's mouth gaped open, then she snapped it shut again, scarcely able to believe her good fortune. "Oh ma'am...I mean Mrs DeVere...you won't regret it, I promise. Let me go and tell Dulcie. This is the best Christmas present we could have ever wished for!"

Evelyn DeVere sighed contentedly. "You know what Florence, I think you're quite right. Making you happy has made me feel more positive than I've been for days. It's quite remarkable." She pulled her leather gloves back on and straightened her cape, brightening as she saw Mr Samuel returning. "Between you and me, normally these inspections bore me to tears," she added, giving Florence a conspiratorial smile. "And like I said, I do find this time of year especially difficult. Meeting you has quite cheered me up...you're a forthright little thing, that's for sure."

"But what about Mr Collier? Won't he be cross that we're going? I don't want to get into more trouble." Florence darted a look at Mr Samuel as he sat at his desk.

"Don't worry about telling Mr Collier, I'll take care of everything. Run along and fetch your belongings. I'll send our coachman Mr Sawley to collect you as soon as I get home. We may as well get you settled in today; there's no time like the present."

CHAPTER 5

"What *exactly* did you say to Mrs DeVere?" Mr Collier demanded angrily. "Never in all my born days has something like this happened. If Mr DeVere had more gumption, he wouldn't allow his wife to rule the roost in such a way, undermining my authority and taking two of my workers from under my nose, just like that."

Florence lowered her gaze, but not before she had seen a glint of amusement in Mr Samuel's eyes. He was enjoying seeing Mr Collier being taken down a peg or two and he paused in his filing task behind Mr Collier's back to make sure he didn't miss a word.

"I didn't say anything I shouldn't have, Mr Collier. All I did was be kind to Mrs DeVere."

"And what makes you think she would want kindness from a lowly worker like you?"

"She was upset, and I remembered what the vicar said in last week's sermon." She risked a glance at Dulcie who was staring down at the toes of her boots and clutching her bandaged hand. "Be kind and compassionate to one another... that's what the vicar told us to do." Florence gulped and let the words hang in the air, wondering whether Collier was about to clout her around the ear like Matron used to. She didn't think she could bear it if Mr Collier snatched this opportunity to leave Thruppley Mill away from them.

Mr Samuel cleared his throat. "We have several new children starting later this week from the orphanage, Mr Collier," he ventured. "They're both fourteen years old and Mrs Ebworth assured me they're quick on their feet and hard working."

Mr Collier thrust his hands into his pockets, tamping down the urge to take the birch to both of the girls. It wouldn't do to send them into the DeVere household with their hands covered in fresh welts, especially as Mrs DeVere had a reputation for being a supporter of reformation for the poor.

"Very well then. I won't stand in your way." Collier puffed out his chest, full of self-pride at his view of himself as a magnanimous person. "You may do as Mrs DeVere requested," he added airily, as though the decision had been his. He glanced out of the window, noticing Mr Sawley pulling his horse and cart to a halt on the snow-crusted yard in front of the office.

Mr Samuel gave the girls a small wink and pulled the thick ledger containing records of their employees towards him. "Shall I enter them both as having left the mill or being on a temporary break, Mr Collier?" He dipped his nib into the inkwell and held it poised over the paper, ready to determine the girls' future with a stroke of his pen.

Collier harrumphed and gave Florence a cold stare. "This is a one-way ticket for you, young lady. I've had more than enough of your disruptive manner. Consider yourselves both formally dismissed from Thruppley Mill...for good." He couldn't resist one final jibe. "And once Mrs DeVere regrets her decision to take you on as maids...which she will within a week, you mark my words...you can go begging on the streets for all I care. My hands are washed of this whole dreadful saga, Florence May...you and your hoity-toity ways can be gone, and good riddance."

With a toss of his head, Mr Collier stomped out of the room, slamming the door behind him and Mr Samuel signed the records with a flourish.

"Well done girls. You made it out of here in one piece," he muttered with a wry smile. "It's not often Mr Collier meets his match. You'll go far, young Florence." He tapped the side of his nose, knowingly and nodded for them to leave. "Just don't muck it up at Bisley Court. This is your chance for a better life that not many of the children who come from the orphanage get, so make the most of it."

Dulcie and Florence swung the outer door open just as a glimmer of sun pierced the clouds, creating a pathway of light towards the entrance. "Look, it's like a sign from heaven, Dulcie. We're out of here!"

"It is! It's a miracle, that's what it is." Dulcie turned to her and giggled.

"Farewell girls. You'd better be on your way before anyone changes their mind."

"Not on your nelly, Mr Samuel. We're leaving

and that's that." Florence darted back into the office, dropping her small bag on the floor and throwing her arms around Mr Samuel, much to his surprise. "Thank you, Sir! You're one of the good ones here. Merry Christmas to you!" She snatched up her bag again and ran down the steps, whooping with joy, and leaving Mr Samuel watching on with a broad smile.

* * *

THE CART TRUNDLED along the road, following the natural course of the river that wound its way through the steep-sided valley. Thankfully the snow had eased and the sun was making a tentative appearance. On either side, honey-coloured stone cottages were ranked in rows, with woodsmoke drifting upwards from their chimneys in the crisp winter air. Higher up on the hillsides, the cottages gave way to common grazing ground, dotted with sheep. Crows gathered in the bare branches of the spinneys of oak and beech trees and their harsh cawing echoed across the land as they squabbled.

"Not much further now." Mr Sawley turned round from the seat at the front of the cart and gave the girls a cheerful smile. "Our Bluebell can do this route in 'er sleep, so it's a nice easy trip for me today." The broad rump of the heavy piebald horse bobbed up and down in the leather traces of her harness as she clopped along the road, and plumes of condensation puffed from her nostrils with each breath she took.

"I'm still pinching myself, Florence. I can't believe our luck. One minute we're waiting for another punishment from Mr Collier, and the next, we're on our way to Bisley Court." Dulcie sounded giddy with excitement and she squeezed Florence's arm again.

"It's like all our prayers have been answered," Florence agreed. "What do you think the house will be like? Mrs DeVere was dressed in such a beautiful gown, with a fur-trimmed cape; she looked like royalty." She sighed happily, picturing a castle in her mind that she had once seen in a storybook.

"Bisley Court is a grand place, alright," Mr Sawley replied over his shoulder. "Mr DeVere inherited it from his father before him, along with the mill. Mind you, grandness doesn't necessarily make for happiness," he added in a low mutter to himself.

"Whoa there Bluebell." A few moments later they reached a bend in the road and Mr Sawley guided the cart through the gateway, giving them the first glimpse of their new home. There were large stone gate posts on either side of the drive and a generously proportioned gatehouse just inside, made from the same mellow stone of the main house. The long driveway was flanked by rhododendron bushes and swept in an elegant curve to the front of the house.

"It's like something out of a dream," Dulcie gasped, trying to take it all in. Her eyes shone with excitement.

Florence nodded in agreement, feeling a flutter of anticipation in her stomach. The house had an imposing frontage, with tall windows that glinted in the low winter sun and wide steps leading up to the large front door. Off to one side, there was a walled kitchen garden, where she could see several gardeners hard at work. On the other side, there was a cluster of buildings that looked to be a coach house and stable block plus a small courtyard with what she presumed was the dairy, laundry, and other buildings that would be needed to keep a grand house like Bisley Court running smoothly.

As Mr Sawley pulled the cart to a stop in front

of the stables a young lad darted out to take Bluebell's reins. "This 'ere is my son, Tom," Sawley informed them.

"Afternoon to you, ladies." Tom peered around the horse and lifted his cap, grinning up at them both. "Pa said we had two new maids joining the household." He stroked the horse's neck and started to uncouple her from the shafts of the cart. "I've been working here for a year already, so if you need to know anything, just ask."

Mr Sawley chuckled as he helped Florence and Dulcie down. "What Tom means to say is that he's only ten years old and still wet behind the ears, with a lot to learn, but he's a bit ahead of you if that helps." He tousled his son's hair to show that his words were good-natured. "He's got a way with animals, has Tom, so he prefers to earn his keep in the stable rather than sitting doing book learning. He kept playing truant from the village school, so in the end, I gave in and the Mrs DeVere said he could start his apprenticeship to become a groom."

"Well, it's nice to have a couple of friends here already, thank you Mr Sawley." Florence took Dulcie's arm. "Where should we go now?"

"Mrs Moore, the housekeeper is expecting you,

I believe. If you walk through the courtyard, you'll see a red door which will take you into the kitchen. Mary Williams the cook will be there and she'll sort you out."

Florence and Dulcie followed his instructions, taking care not to slip on the path where the snow had an icy crust where the sun hadn't reached it.

"Do you think we'll be working together?" Dulcie asked anxiously. "I know you said Mrs DeVere said she only had one position to fill...I'm ever so grateful you persuaded her to take me too, Florence."

They arrived at the steps that led up to the kitchen and Florence gave her lifelong friend a quick hug, sensing that she was nervous. "Of course I wouldn't have left without you, Dulcie. We're like family, remember. You and me...together since we were babies." She took a deep breath and stood up straighter. "Right, come on. Let's show 'em what we're made of."

Suddenly the door sprang open in front of them and a plump face peered out. "Are you the two girls from Thruppley Mill?" The door opened wider. "Don't stand there freezing to death, come on in." The woman gave them a broad smile. "I'm Mary Williams, the cook. Let me get you a nice cup of tea before Mrs Moore finds you. She's got a sharp tongue that one and I reckon she got out of bed on the wrong side this morning."

Florence and Dulcie sipped gratefully on the milky tea that Cook had poured for them and she kept up a steady stream of conversation as she bustled around the large scrubbed table at the centre of the cavernous kitchen. Rows of gleaming copper pots hung from a wooden rack over the range and a huge pan of stew bubbled on the hotplate, making their mouths water.

"That last maid turned out to be a proper flibbertigibbet. She took a liking to the boy who delivers coal and the next thing we know, she's expecting his baby and then she upped and left in the middle of the night. 'Twas quite shameful, the whole affair, so mind you don't go the same way." She paused and eyed them up. "You're pretty girls, both of you, so don't fall for any flattery from the village boys."

Dulcie nodded hastily. "Of course we won't. We're used to ignoring unwanted advances anyway. Mr Collier didn't hold with that sort of thing happening at the mill."

The cook heaved a pan of drained boiled potatoes onto the table and added butter and milk, before starting to mash them.

"The main rule to remember at Bisley Court is to do as you're told...that goes without saying. And when Mrs DeVere has one of her sad days, you have to be extra careful not to do anything to annoy Mr DeVere."

Florence finished her tea and quickly washed both of their cups up. "Why is Mrs DeVere sad at this time of year?" she asked curiously.

"Oh...it was something that happened a very long time ago. There was a fire and Mrs DeVere lost one of her boys when he was just a tot. She never got over it and—"

"Ah, here you are." A tall thin woman swept into the kitchen and gave Cook a disapproving frown. "I hope you're not gossiping, Mrs Williams. We don't like to air Bisley Court's tragic past to all and sundry, do we," she snapped. She turned her gaze on Florence and Dulcie. "I'm Mrs Moore, the housekeeper and Mrs DeVere has instructed me to tell you what your positions are.

"Thank you Mrs Moore," Florence replied. "Cook very kindly gave us a cup of tea, but we're ready to start work just as soon as you say."

Florence looked at the two women who they

would now be answering to instead of Mr Collier. They made a curious pair. Where Cook was plump and jolly, Mrs Moore was angular and stern, even down to her pursed lips and beady gaze that seemed determined to find fault wherever she looked.

"I'm not sure a cup of tea was really necessary," Mrs Moore said with a disapproving sniff. "We don't encourage idleness, and you'll take your breaks with the rest of the staff at the allotted times in future."

Cook sighed noisily. "Have a care, Mrs Moore. It's freezing outside and Florence just told me that young Dulcie here almost lost her arm in one of the looms at the mill this morning. A cup of tea isn't exactly breaking the rules, is it? Let the poor things have ten minutes to find their feet before you start telling them off."

"Standards, Cook. We must maintain standards and after that fiasco with the last maid, I shall be keeping a very close eye on things. Gather up your belongings and follow me please." Mrs Moore stuck her nose in the air and sailed back out of the kitchen with brisk steps that echoed on the stone floor with efficient authority.

Cook shook her head and gave Florence a

sympathetic smile. "Don't mind Mrs Moore," she said quickly. "Her bark is worse than her bite, especially at this time of year when everyone is a little on edge. We've both been with the DeVere's since before...before it happened you see. We can remember when the house was a happier place, that's all." Florence and Dulcie hastily picked up their bags to hurry after the housekeeper. "If you do a good job, and watch your manners, you'll find she's alright," Cook added, shooing them on their way.

Florence darted a look at Dulcie as they hastened down the corridor to where the formidable housekeeper was tapping her foot impatiently.

I hope to goodness we're not about to find out that it's worse here than at the mill. The thought that Mrs Moore seemed rather like the dreadful Mr Collier in her demeanour made Florence feel a shiver of worry.

"Do you think she's cross with us already?" Dulcie whispered.

"Of course not," Florence muttered back. "We survived Matron and the mill. I'm sure it will be much nicer here. We'll be fine." She squared her shoulders and tried to look on the bright side. So far, everyone apart from Mrs Moore had been kind and welcoming and she felt sure that once they both got into the rhythm of their new positions, they would be able to show the housekeeper that they wanted to be a valued part of the Bisley Court household.

CHAPTER 6

"Make sure your apron is straight and then you may serve the toast." Mrs Moore walked around Florence with her arms crossed, giving her one last inspection through critical eyes before nodding that she could go.

Florence hurried down the corridor, smoothing down her crisply starched apron over the black dress that swished around her ankles. The clothes felt stiff and cumbersome after the softness of the threadbare dress she had worn at the mill and the mobcap that perched on her curls seemed determined to slip to one side every time she moved. She secured it more firmly with a hairpin and turned into the kitchen, taking an appreciative sniff of the tantalising aromas that were already coming from the top oven of the range. Clearly, Cook had already been hard at work for several hours while she had been sweeping and polishing the upstairs landing with Penelope, the eight-year-old slavey who had started a couple of weeks earlier.

"You've passed the first test with Mrs Moore then, have you?" Cook gave her a friendly smile as she pushed the tray containing freshly toasted bread standing to attention in two silver toast racks towards Florence. "Take this to the dining room and put them on the table. Then check that there's enough jam and marmalade in the bowls."

"Yes, Cook. And should I just wait in the dining room, or come back afterwards?" Florence's mouth felt dry with nerves and she swallowed, hoping her trepidation wouldn't show.

"Wait there in case they want more toast and Sally will tell you what to do. Don't stand too close to the table, mind. It's not the done thing to make your employers feel as though you're hovering and listening to their conversation."

A moment later, Florence edged into the dining room and Sally, one of the more experienced maids, jerked her head towards the polished sideboard, showing her where to put the tray. Florence placed it carefully down, then carried the two toast racks to the table where the family was sitting.

"Some toast for you Mrs DeVere," Florence whispered.

Her new employer gave her a brief but encouraging smile, but as Florence backed away to take her place discreetly at the edge of the room, she saw her expression cloud with sadness again.

"I'm not entirely sure Mr Collier has grasped the gravity of the situation," Mr DeVere muttered, shaking his head. He slathered butter onto a piece of toast, then added some jam, before taking a bite and chewing it briskly. "If we don't work more efficiently, we'll never be able to compete, it's a simple as that."

"I'm sure you'll know what to do to make it right, dear." Evelyn DeVere sighed faintly and sipped her tea.

"It hasn't helped, you taking on two of the employees from the mill. Collier really was most agitated about that."

Florence jumped as she realised he was talking about her and Dulcie and Sally turned to look at her with raised eyebrows.

Mrs DeVere put her cup down carefully and

gave her husband a firm look. "I had to replace the last maid and I really don't have the energy to trawl through the village to find someone at this time of year. Besides, Alice needs someone at the gatehouse. She can't be expected to do everything herself, Robert. It wouldn't be right for a woman of her position. Dulcie seems like a sensible girl. She'll suit my sister fine."

Robert DeVere harrumphed with irritation. "That's all well and good, Evelyn, but I'm not running a charity here. Please remember that. We don't need any more waifs and strays and people who don't pull their weight in the household. It's bad enough—"

"Oh, Robert!" Evelyn interrupted. "My sister has nobody else since her husband died, so letting her stay at the gatehouse is the least we can do." Evelyn's cheeks flushed at the sting of her husband's words. "And all this talk of people not pulling their weight...I do hope you're not refer-ring to—"

Before she could finish her sentence, the dining room door creaked open tentatively.

"Don't just stand there dithering, boy. Come and eat your breakfast. You need to build up your energy if I'm going to train you up in the business."

Mr DeVere glared at the person in the doorway, his irritation mounting.

Florence watched as a pale young man stepped into the room and slid into the seat on the opposite side of the table. He had the same blonde hair as Evelyn, although hers was fading to grey and she realised he must be their son. Everything about him seemed nervous and apologetic, and he blinked rapidly as his father cast his stern gaze towards him.

"I'm not very hungry, Papa. Maybe I'll just have a cup of tea this morning."

Evelyn gave him a fond smile as Sally sprang forward to pour the tea for him and refill the other cups on the table.

"Poppycock," Robert snapped. "You'll eat a hearty breakfast and take a ride out with me afterwards. I won't tolerate any son of mine languishing upstairs all day like some feeble specimen." He twisted his head and snapped his fingers in Florence's direction.

"You...girl. Being at Bisley Court isn't an excuse for idleness compared to your time at the mill, despite what my wife might have you believe. Serve Master DeVere with some devilled kidneys and scrambled eggs, right away."

Florence jumped to attention and did as she was told, piling up the golden buttery eggs and rich meat onto a warmed plate, before carrying it carefully to the table. "There you are, Sir. Is there anything else you'd like? Some water, perhaps?"

Miles looked embarrassed at his father's barked instruction and shot her a grateful look with a nod. "Thank you, that would be nice." He picked up his knife and fork and took a small mouthful, forcing it down with a sip of water, shrinking back into his seat under the weight of his father's stare.

"I...I'm not sure I'm well enough to ride today, Papa. I didn't sleep very well and it looks very cold outside."

"Oh for goodness sake." Robert drained the rest of his tea, then blotted his moustache with his napkin before throwing it down on the table. "You do try my patience, Miles. Some days I wish it had—"

"Stop it," Evelyn said sharply. "Miles can't help having weak lungs. Once the weather becomes warmer again he'll get stronger, I'm sure of it."

Robert stood up and buttoned his morning coat. "Well, I for one have got work to do if we're to keep the mill profitable. Make sure the boy does something useful with his time, Evelyn. I'm determined the DeVere family name won't come to nothing; not after all my hard work, and my father's before me. Although on days like this, I wonder why I bother." He sighed loudly, signalling his frustration with everyone in the room and hurried away to his study.

* * *

By mid-morning, Florence had mastered the skill of keeping her mobcap straight and was standing in the chilly scullery plucking pheasants ready for the terrine that Cook would be making later that day. Ten birds had been hung up from the rafters by Tom, who had scampered up the step ladder as though he'd done it a dozen times before. "Use the blunt side of the knife to get the stubbly feathers out, else you'll rip the flesh," he had advised her with a cheerful grin. "Pa used to catch the odd bird for us when I was a nipper before Ma died. She taught me how to do a proper good job preparing them. It's making my mouth water just thinking about the tasty pheasant stews she used to make."

Florence brushed a lock of hair from her forehead and pulled out another tuft of feathers, revealing the dimpled skin beneath.

"Make sure you separate the feathers properly, Penelope. Mrs DeVere lets us sell the prettiest ones to the milliner in Gloucester for making hat decorations. I'm saving up the money for us to spend at the summer fayre next year." Cook bustled through from the kitchen to check they were doing everything to her liking and the downy feathers eddied across the floor in the swish of her skirt. "That looks grand," she added. "We'll be having goose and ham on Christmas Day, but Master Miles is very fond of my pheasant terrine so I always like to make sure we have at least one for him.

"I hope there's enough for us to try a bit," Penelope mumbled as she scrabbled on the floor for the last feathers which had floated down in front of her. "I ain't never had a proper Christmas dinner before. My Pa used to say it was a waste of good beer money. Before he was sent to jail, anyway. I used to dream about having a feast." Her stomach rumbled and she giggled.

"Well, I'm sure you'll enjoy our dinner then Penelope," Cook replied. "It's nothing too grand, but Mrs DeVere lets us have an evening off to enjoy ourselves and Mr Sawley puts a tree up for us in the corner of the servants' hall."

Penelope's eyes lit up and Florence was struck by a sudden thought. "Do you think Dulcie will be able to join us, Cook? I know she's going to be busy at the gatehouse with Mrs DeVere's sister most of the time, but she's quite shy and I must confess I do miss her. I'm worried she might not make any new friends down there. We've always been together, you see. We look out for each other, always have done."

"I expect so, dear. Mrs Sherringham was widowed earlier this year, and the DeVeres are her only family now, so I'm sure she will join them for Christmas Day. Other than that, you'll probably see Dulcie on Sundays at church, and if she gets sent up here on errands. Mrs Sherringham often comes to the main house to dine with her sister, so I'll suggest to Mrs Moore that Dulcie could eat with all of us whenever that happens."

Florence finished the last bird and washed her hands in the sink with a scrubbing brush. Now that she knew she would see Dulcie regularly it was a load off her mind. Although Mrs Sherringham sounded nice enough, she had spent most of the night fretting that Dulcie would feel lonely, away from all the other servants of Bisley Court.

"Now then...Mrs Moore has gone into

Chalsworth to do some shopping ahead of the festive season. Even though the family don't like to make a big fuss at this time of year, you'd be surprised how busy we get once Christmas gets closer." Cook peered into the cavernous larder deciding what to do next.

"Penelope, you can peel the potatoes. Florence, I'd like you to take some fruit cake and coffee up for Master Miles. The poor boy is wasting away up there, pining for his brother." She shook her head sorrowfully and hurried away to prepare the coffee before Florence had a chance to ask her any more about what had happened to the brother.

Florence carried the tray up the grand staircase under the butler's watchful eye. The walls were lined with ornately framed paintings of hunting scenes and stern-gazed gentlemen who she thought must be family members from previous generations. It felt as though they were watching her every move and she took extra care not to trip over the hem of her dress.

"Turn right at the top, follow the corridor to the very end, then it's the second door on the left next to the glass-fronted bookcase." Florence muttered the instructions that Cook had given her. The top landing was generously proportioned and she paused for a moment at the surprising sight of a tall cabinet full of stuffed birds. From blue-winged jays to iridescent starlings, she had never seen anything so curious in her life; they looked so lifelike and she wished she had time to study them more closely.

"Run along, Florence. You don't want to keep Master Miles waiting." Ernest Middleton, the family's aged butler called up the stairs to chivy her along, confirming Florence's suspicion that everyone was keeping a close eye on her performance.

A moment later, she placed the tray on the inlaid walnut occasional table in the corridor and tapped lightly on what she hoped was the correct door.

"Come in." The voice sounded guarded.

"Cook asked me to bring you some cake and coffee." Florence edged through the door, pushing it wider with her foot so she wouldn't bump the tray.

"Leave it over there. I'm not really hungry."

"But you hardly ate any breakfast, Sir, you must be starving." The words popped out before Florence could stop herself. "I...I mean...I'm sorry

Sir, but it does smell very good. You wouldn't have to ask me twice to eat it."

Miles stood up from the armchair next to the window and chuckled. "Are you always this impertinent. The last maid never said a word, yet here you are, telling me what to do on your first day here."

"Oh no, Sir. I'm sorry. I forgot myself. I didn't mean to speak out of turn." Florence blushed and bobbed a curtsey, before scuttling for the door to leave.

"Wait a minute," Miles called, beckoning her back into the room. "What's your name? I'm Miles DeVere."

"Florence, Sir. Florence May. Like you said, I've only just started working here so please forgive me if I make a mistake or two. I'll try hard not to, but sometimes I get ahead of myself." She giggled nervously, hoping that she hadn't offended him already.

"Please don't call me Sir, Florence. You make me sound as though I'm a hundred years old. You can call me Miles."

"I can't do that, Sir...I mean Miles...I mean Master DeVere. It wouldn't be right at all, what with me being a servant and you being Mr

DeVere's son." Although she had never worked in service, Florence knew that maids were not allowed to be friends with their employers. She darted a look at him and was surprised to see that he looked slightly crestfallen.

Miles picked up the fruitcake and looked at it, before returning it to the plate and flopping back into the armchair again. "I insist, Florence. At least, it's alright to call me Miles when it's just us in the room. It's fine as long as my parents don't hear." He gave her a conspiratorial grin.

"Here, Cook made this coffee freshly for you." She poured the coffee out and the room filled with the rich, nutty aroma of it.

"Oh alright then. I'll eat the cake to keep Cook happy. As long as you share it with me, Florence. She doesn't like it if I send her food back uneaten." He broke a piece off and munched on it unenthusiastically, pushing the remainder towards her. "Please, I know it's not the usual thing to do, but you'd be helping me out."

Suddenly he was seized with a coughing fit that made his shoulders convulse. "I...I can't breathe," he gasped, snatching at his collar to loosen it. His eyes watered and a faint sheen of sweat coated his brow.

"Sit up, Miles." Florence sprang forward to assist, hitching him upright in the chair. She leant him over his knees and thumped him on his back several times, horrified that he might choke to death in front of her eyes.

"I...I'm alright now." The coughing subsided and the room was filled with the harsh sound of wheezing. Every breath looked like a struggle and he leant back in the chair again, closing his eyes with a pained expression.

"Lawks, you gave me a fright there. It must have been a bit of cake caught in your throat." Florence shook out a blanket and folded it, placing it carefully over his knees. Looking more closely at him, she could see that his complexion had a grey pallor and the bones of his wrists jutted out.

Miles opened his eyes again and gave her an apologetic smile. "No, it's not the cake. I'm just a weakling, Florence. My lungs never recovered from the accident. Now you can see why I'm such a disappointment to my Papa."

"Don't say that," Florence said hastily. "I'm sure your Papa is very fond of you...even if he did sound a bit short this morning. Anyway, it's hardly your fault if this weather makes you unwell," she added stoutly.

"You're very kind, Florence, but sadly also wrong. I can see it in his eyes...he wishes it was me who was lost when we were babies...not my brother Hugo." Miles pulled the rug higher and shivered. "I've got used to it over the years, but it's always worse as autumn turns into winter. That's when Hugo perished, and by a cruel irony, it's when my health is always at its worst."

"I don't believe it can be true," Florence replied, looking puzzled. "You and your parents live in this beautiful house, with everything you could possibly wish for."

Miles glanced around, seeing Bisley Court through Florence's eyes. The sumptuous fabric of the curtains and bedding, the crackling fire in the hearth, and the rolling grounds of the estate as far as they could see. He shrugged guiltily. "You'd think we'd be happy, wouldn't you? But none of us seems to be able to escape the shadow of what happened in the past, even though I wish we could. Sometimes I think Papa wishes I'd never been born."

CHAPTER 7

lorence couldn't help feeling shocked at what Miles had just said so casually. "That can't be right, surely?" She poured Miles a fresh cup of coffee and handed it to him now that the coughing had stopped.

"I wish it wasn't the case...but I don't think Papa will ever be proud of me. I mean, what is there to be proud of," he added with a hint of bitterness, gesturing at his ailing body.

Florence riddled the fire and added some fresh logs which crackled comfortingly, filling the room with the scent of applewood. It had started to snow again outside and the winter wind rattled the windows of his room. She could feel the draught around her ankles, so it probably wasn't helping Miles feel any better.

"What happened...to your brother? Your mama looked sad this morning. You must miss him terribly."

Miles sipped on the coffee and ate another bite of the fruitcake, and she was pleased to see that a hint of colour returning to his cheeks.

"I don't remember him. I'm a twin and Hugo was my twin brother. I only know what happened from snatches of conversation. My Mama finds it too painful to talk about."

"A twin? You must feel as though there's a part of you missing?" Florence's heart squeezed with sympathy for the sadness which must have hung over the family all these years.

"When we were about six months old, the house was being refurbished so we were living in a house that Papa owned in Chalsworth, just while the work was taking place. Mama and Papa had gone to Captain Mellrose's for a winter ball. Then while they were out, there was a fire at the house. Everyone said that the maid who looked after us did her best, but the house burnt to the ground. She managed to save me...but my brother was never found. Mama and Papa could only assume that Hugo perished in the fire."

"That's terrible." Florence paused from her task, wanting to give Miles her full attention.

"We weren't identical twins, but you're right, I do miss him even though I have no memory of him. It would have been nice to have a brother to share my life with." Miles struggled to his feet and opened one of the small drawers of his escritoire, pulling out a piece of paper. He handed it to Florence. "This was a sketch one of Mama's friends did of us for a painting Mama commissioned. It's the only thing I have to remember Hugo by."

Florence took it and turned it to the light. The softly pencilled lines and watercoloured wash showed two babies on a chair. Although there were similarities, she could see that one was fairer than the other and their face shapes were different. She patted Miles's arm, filled with sympathy for him, before realising that it was inappropriate.

"I...I'm sorry, I didn't mean to be forward." She hastily handed back the sketch and turned to sweep up the ash from the hearth to cover her blunder.

"Don't apologise for being kind," Miles replied with a rueful smile. "It's nice that I can talk about what happened with someone. Usually, it's never mentioned, but Mama does find this time of year hard because it reminds her of what happened."

"It must be hard for your father too," Florence said tentatively. "Do you have any other brothers or sisters?"

Miles's face clouded. "I once heard him in a fine temper, saying that Mama was as much of a disappointment as me because she could never bear him any more children."

Florence gasped at the cruelty of the words, and she started to understand why Miles had said what he had.

"I never knew my parents," she confided. "I was at Chalsworth Orphanage, and then I got sent to work at your father's mill. I always wondered what it would have been like to grow up in a proper family."

"You must think I'm very spoiled then," Miles replied. He gestured at the comfortable room around him. "I live a life of luxury, but all I really want is to make Papa proud of me." He gave Florence a sudden smile. "This has been the best day I've had for ages. You're much more fun than most of the maids. Perhaps you could come up another day and we can talk...you can tell me about life in the orphanage perhaps?"

Florence grinned. "Tell you about the dreadful Matron Ebworth? Some of what she used to do to us would make you see things a bit differently, that's for sure." She picked up the bucket of ash. "I don't mind talking to you a bit, but only if it doesn't distract me from my work."

Miles nodded. "As you wish. I was just being friendly." He picked up a book, signalling that his mind was already elsewhere, so Florence let herself out.

As she hurried towards the back stairs to take the ash away, Sally watched her from the shadows where she was dusting. Her eyes narrowed thoughtfully as she glanced at the grandfather clock in the corner, noting that Florence had taken longer than needed to deliver the food to Miles. She squirrelled the information away at the back of her mind. It never harmed to have a bit of gossip about the other maids that might come in useful one day, she told herself with the hint of a smile.

"Where have you been all this time?" Cook looked up from the cake mix she was beating in a large bowl. Her sleeves were rolled up and her cheeks were bright pink from the exertion.

"Sorry, Cook. Miles was taken ill with a coughing fit and then he wanted to chat. It seemed rude to leave him." Florence scurried to the sink to make a start on washing up the dirty dishes that Cook had pointed to.

"Miles? Don't you mean *Master* Miles?" Cook stopped what she was doing and gave Florence a shrewd look. The girl's chestnut curls and the dusting of freckles over her rosy cheeks would be enough to turn heads when she was older, she thought to herself. And there was something about the frank way that Florence spoke that might attract the wrong kind of attention.

"Oh...yes, sorry Cook. I meant Master Miles."

Cook scraped the cake mix into the awaiting tin and slid it into the oven, before bringing the bowl to the sink. "Don't ever make the mistake of thinking you're equal to Master Miles, Florence, no matter how much he wants to be your friend." She gave the girl an earnest look, seeing the blush creeping up her cheeks. "If you had a Ma, you'd know about these things, but seeing as you don't, take it from me...you're a servant. Miles is a kind boy, but he will always be your master. You can't be friends and if you try, it will end in heartache. Mr DeVere wouldn't hesitate to throw you out without a reference if he thought Miles was liaising inappropriately with someone as lowly as a maid."

"I was just trying to help him, that's all," Florence protested. "I thought he was going to choke to death." She scrubbed the custard from the bottom of the saucepan in front of her with renewed vigour, trying to make amends.

Cook smiled at her to show that she meant no harm. "All I'm saying is remember your place, Florence. One day Miles will own all this, and his father wants him to take over the mill. He needs to learn about the business, not have his head turned by a pretty girl who works for the family. Don't let your kindness be mistaken for anything else, otherwise Mrs Moore will make your life a misery." She nudged Florence with a grin. "Besides, you're a good little worker and I need all the help I can get if we're going to give the family a wonderful Christmas...even if they think they don't much want to bother with all that."

Florence nodded, grateful for Cook's advice. Miles had looked so forlorn when he had told her about the fire and Hugo's death, that she had wanted to comfort him. But Cook was right. She couldn't risk losing this job and she was determined not to. Dulcie would be devastated if they got split up because of her careless behaviour.

He doesn't seem to have many friends though...not like me and Dulcie. Is it really so wrong to be friendly with someone who's lonely like that? The thoughts buzzed in her mind, leaving her feeling confused. As she worked her way through the dirty dishes, she considered what Miles had said just before she left. He had told her that many years ago there had been a rumour in Chalsworth that the fire had been started deliberately. She shivered. Who would want to do such a thing? And what if they still lived in Chalsworth?

"You can get started on peeling the vegetables when you've finished that lot." Cook plonked a basket full of potatoes and swedes, still covered in mud, by her elbow and bustled away.

"Yes, Cook, of course." Florence stifled a yawn and lifted her shoulders to ease her aching muscles, thinking back to her conversation with Miles. She felt torn. Even though she had only just arrived at the house, she had sensed that Miles lived almost like a recluse, trapped in the house by the weak lungs that he had told her were a legacy of the fire. Life was passing him by and she wondered why Mr DeVere was so cruel with his words to the only child he had left. Her natural inclination was to be friendly, but she couldn't risk being his friend, no matter if that was what he wanted. She decided she would tell him the next time she saw him, and hope that he would understand her reasoning. She had a lot to learn about being a maid, but it was a hundred times better than the noise and choking air of the mill. Bisley Court was her new life and she was determined to make the most of this opportunity, just like Mr Samuel had advised.

* * *

By the time she had been there a couple of weeks, Florence felt as though she was settling in well and the mill was starting to become like a distant memory that she could put behind her.

The bell on the wall jangled insistently and Florence glanced up, seeing that it was for the dining room. Without needing to be asked, she quickly put fresh tea and toast on a tray and hurried away. As she entered the room, the aroma of kedgeree wafted from the silver serving dish on the sideboard and a fire crackled in the hearth, giving it a cosy feel. Sally was already serving up the savoury food and Florence gave her a smile, hoping that she might win her friendship, although the senior maid seemed as distant as ever.

"I need to visit the tenants later this morning. Would you like to come with me, Miles?" Evelyn smiled at her son, hoping to encourage him to come outside. "I can make sure Mr Sawley puts plenty of blankets in the carriage. It might do you good to get some fresh air."

"If you'd like me to, Mama, it would be my pleasure." Miles still sounded wheezy to Florence and she noticed that since his father had strode in to join them for breakfast he was trying not to cough.

"Visiting the tenants, you say?" Mr DeVere peered over the top of his newspaper. "Isn't that what I pay Reginald for? He's the estate steward, so it's up to him to collect the rent from everyone."

"I'm not collecting the rent, Robert, don't worry. I know some of the tenants have had a difficult time with illnesses and suchlike this year. I thought it would be nice to take a few small gifts for them...Cook has baked some extra cakes and

Sawley has made up some small bundles of kindling wood. I purchased a few small trinkets for the children as well—"

"Really, Evelyn. I said last year that you weren't to spoil them, didn't I?" Robert folded up his newspaper and laid it on the table. "These people will take advantage of your good nature if you're not careful. They have a roof over their heads and work on the estate. If some of the wives are struggling because their husbands spend all their money in The Old Oak Tavern, that's none of our business."

Miles caught Florence's eye and cleared his throat, signalling that he would like more tea. "Don't you think times are changing Papa? Surely people in our position should take better care of our tenants and workers. It's thanks to their hard work that we live so well. I think it's a nice idea, what Mama has suggested. Besides, I'm sure it doesn't cost us much to show them our appreciation for Christmas."

Florence poured the tea carefully into Miles's cup. As she did so, she noticed that Robert's was empty as well, so she glided discreetly around the table, wanting to be there ready for when he called for more himself.

"You're just as bad as your mother," Robert suddenly snapped. "If you made an effort to learn about what really goes into keeping the mill going you would understand. And it's the same with the estate." His face darkened as he warmed to his theme. "The people I employ don't deserve to be mollycoddled with gifts and given time off. In my father's day, they were jolly grateful to have a job and a home, and they knew their place."

"But Robert, old Mrs Crouch was widowed and she has five children to feed. And what about the Burton family? Since Alf Burton was injured on the farm last year, they've been struggling to make ends meet."

"Now that you bring them up, you've reminded me. This will be their last Christmas on the estate. They've missed their rent twice, so Reginald will be evicting them in the new year." Robert's moustache bristled with indignation when he saw Evelyn's look of dismay.

"That's not the way to treat them, Papa. Mr Crouch has worked on the farm since he was a boy. And the Burtons too. If you evict them, they'll probably end up in the workhouse." Miles looked horrified.

"Not the workhouse, it's dreadful there." The

words came out of Florence's mouth before she could stop them. "S...sorry, Sir, what I meant was, would you like more tea?" Florence hovered next to Robert, not knowing whether to pour the tea or not.

"Tea? What are you talking about, girl?" Robert glared at Florence. "Are you being impertinent?"

Florence stumbled backwards and the tea slopped from the teapot, splashing on Robert's coat.

"Look what you've done," he roared. He stood up, brushing the scalding liquid from his arm. "Miles, don't you dare question my business decisions again like that. You're nothing but a disappointment to me. When you've decided you're ready to knuckle down and learn about the business, I might listen to you. But until then, stay out of my sight."

He barged past Florence, almost knocking her over. "I'm terribly sorry, Sir, I didn't mean to spill the tea on you."

Robert stopped again and glared at her. "I don't know what's got into Miles, but I hope you're not being a bad influence. You'll be out on the streets faster than your feet can touch the ground if I think you've been turning his head. It's bad enough having to deal with my wife's liberal notions, let alone my servants getting above their station."

"N...no, Sir. I'm not being a bad influence, I promise..." Florence stuttered.

The door slammed behind Robert just as Evelyn burst into tears and hurried from the room, hastily followed by Miles.

"You'd better lookout," Sally said sourly from where she had been watching from the corner of the room. "Once you get on the wrong side of Mr DeVere, there's no telling what might happen. And don't think you're anything special, missy. I've seen the way you make eyes at him. Master Miles might think you're his friend, but you've only been here two minutes." She gave Florence a thin smile that didn't reach her eyes. "If anyone is going to be his friend, it should be me, not a scruffy orphan who washed up here from the mill. I know what you're up to, and it won't end well for you, you mark my words."

"I don't know what you mean," Florence replied hotly. I'm not up to anything, other than trying to work hard and be polite and friendly to the DeVere family." She felt a wave of shame wash through her that Sally thought she was trying to make trouble in the house.

"So you say. But I've been noticing things, Florence. A word to Mrs Moore is all it would take for you to be sent packing." Sally gave her a sly smile, enjoying her moment of power. "There's a right way and a wrong way to fit in at Bisley Court. You need to remember that you're at the bottom of the pile, where you belong. Along with poor little Penelope." She tossed her head and marched out of the room, leaving Florence wondering whether she would ever be with people who actually wanted her around.

CHAPTER 8

As Florence tidied away the breakfast things in the kitchen, Sally's words lingered in her mind. She felt a shiver of anxiety at the way the maid seemed determined to think the worst of her. Over the last couple of weeks, Florence had taken care to be polite and friendly to Miles, but not to loiter too long when he wanted to talk.

He had assured her that his father took no interest in how he spent his time, but Mr DeVere's outburst over breakfast confirmed that Florence had been right to be cautious.

Suddenly there was a loud clatter as Penelope knocked a saucepan off the table, sending stewed apple all over the floor.

"Goodness me, child. Must you be so clumsy?" Cook glared at her, looking unusually flustered.

"I'll help clear up," Florence said hastily as Penelope started to cry. "It won't take us a minute."

Cook sighed and turned her attention back to the sausages she was making. "I'm sorry Penelope. Dry your tears, I didn't mean to speak harshly."

"S...s...sorry, Cook. I'm trying my hardest, but sometimes I'm all fingers and thumbs. I wish I was as dainty as Florence, but I ain't. I used to get teased something rotten at the orphanage...they used to call me Ponderous Penelope and tell me nobody would ever want me..." Her bottom lip started to wobble again.

"Don't you pay any heed to that," Florence said stoutly. She squeezed the girl's shoulders and handed her a damp cloth. "We've both got plenty to learn, and it's probably because you're still growing that sometimes you drop things, isn't that right Cook?"

Mrs Williams nodded as she turned the handle of the mincer, adding a generous scoop of her herb mix, the exact blend of which was a closely guarded secret. "I'm just feeling a bit flustered

THE MAID'S WINTER WISH

because Mrs Moore has taken to her bed with a nasty cold, right when we're at our busiest," she explained.

Florence and Penelope cleaned the sticky fruit off the floor and it was spick and span again in no time.

"Right Penelope. There's no time like the present to learn something new. I'm going to hold the sausage skins, and I want you to turn this handle to force the meat out." Cook beckoned her over and Penelope grinned as she clambered onto the chair to grasp the handle.

"Shall I take Mrs Moore some of your chicken broth, Cook?" Florence would rather have stayed clear of the housekeeper, but she knew that Cook was struggling to get everything done with Mrs Moore out of action.

Cook paused and ran a stubby finger down her list of tasks for the day. "You know what would help me most? Mrs Moore was going to go into Chalsworth today. That dozy delivery boy forgot to bring the extra flour and suet I ordered. Plus we've almost run out of sugar and tea. I happen to know that Mr Sawley is taking Mrs Sherringham and Dulcie into Chalsworth later this morning. If you could go with them and get the groceries I need, that would help me no end."

Florence felt a surge of excitement. She hadn't seen Dulcie for almost a week and the thought of an outing into Chalsworth felt like an unexpected treat. Better still, it showed her that Cook must trust her which gave her a warm glow of satisfaction.

An hour later, she was squashed up next to Dulcie in the back of the carriage, sitting opposite Mrs Sherringham as they bowled through the lanes towards town. The snow-covered fields looked like pillowy eiderdowns, and the steam rose off the backs of the sheep and cattle as they jostled to reach the sweet mounds of hay the farmers forked into their feeding troughs. Starlings and fieldfares squabbled in the holly trees over the plump red berries and the edge of the river glinted as the pale sun caught the icicles which crusted the reeds like sparkling gemstones.

"It's so beautiful, Mrs Sherringham. We were never allowed out of the orphanage, so we never really knew that all this existed, apart from what people told us. It's like a fairytale." Dulcie's eyes shone with delight and Alice Sherringham smiled at them both.

"It's refreshing to see two youngsters who appreciate what's around them," she replied. "When Mr Sherringham was alive, Lord rest his soul, we lived in Birmingham. Although the shops were far superior to Chalsworth, the snow was never really clean like this because of all the smog from the factories." She took a lace handkerchief from her reticule and dabbed at her eyes which had misted over at the memory of her late husband.

Florence looked at Mrs Sherringham more closely. She was quite unlike her younger sister, Mrs DeVere. Her hair was already greying, and the ringlets under her bonnet bounced every time she spoke. Her faded blue eyes looked nervous behind the glasses which perched owlishly on the end of her nose, and the clothes she favoured were fussy and overly decorative, in an old-fashioned style that made her look like an old woman before her time.

"I don't usually like to come into Chalsworth unless I'm with Mrs DeVere," she confided. Her voice was high and reminded Florence of the little brown sparrows that chirped on the sill of her bedroom window in the attic.

"I'll look out for you, don't worry about a thing

Mrs Sherringham," Dulcie said with a grin. "We'll get the bits and bobs you need and you'll be back in the comfort of your cosy parlour, next to the fire again in no time."

Mrs Sherringham sighed and sat back in the corner of her carriage, plucking the fringe of her shawl. "I do hope there won't be any unsavoury types to contend with," she continued with a shiver. "It's a constant worry for a widow like me. Mr Sherringham used to make sure I always felt safe, but there are ruffians all around these days…"

A few minutes later, Mr Sawley pulled the horse to a halt on the edge of the market square and opened the door for them to dismount. Florence double-checked that the coins Mrs Williams had given her were safely tucked in the pocket under her apron and hurried away, promising she would be back by the time the clock was striking twelve.

Mr Sawley gave the horse a nosebag of oats and stamped his feet to get the warmth back into them. He watched Dulcie carefully shepherding Mrs Sherringham to the dressmakers where she was being fitted for a warmer mourning dress to see her through the winter months.

"Mind out will you." A drayman barged past Florence as she slithered along the pavement, rolling a large barrel of beer ahead of him with ease. The snow was compacted making it slippery and it was busier than she had thought it would be. She glanced at the large clock on the front of the guildhall; by her calculations, he had one hour until she had to be back at the carriage. She smiled to herself, feeling suddenly giddy with the unexpected freedom she had been given. One whole hour without the likes of Matron, Mr Collier, or even Mrs Moore telling her what to do.

"If I'm quick with the groceries, I'll have time to look in the shop windows," she murmured, quickening her pace. She resisted the allure of looking already and weaved through the other shoppers until she was at the general provisions store where Cook had told her to go. The bell tinkled as she let herself in and a tousle-headed young man popped up from behind the counter.

"What can I get you? Ma's just stepped out, so I'm in charge, even though I should be out on my delivery rounds." He looked her up and down and grinned cheerfully.

"Ah, well if you're the delivery boy, it's because of you that I'm here," Florence shot back at him.

"Mrs Williams, the cook at Bisley Court has sent me to get some items which you didn't deliver."

"You've got me there," the young man replied. He held up his hands apologetically. "Our Gertrude lost a shoe and went lame. I was in that much of a bother sorting her out, I clean forgot to put the last few things in Mrs Williams' order." He leaned over the counter and grasped her hand, shaking it enthusiastically. "Norman Crocker at 'yer service. Let me give you a free twist of humbugs to make up for the inconvenience."

Florence chuckled as she read out her list. "It makes a nice change to get out of the house, to be honest. Although I won't say no to the sweets if you're giving them away. My friend Dulcie, who works as a maid at the gatehouse, loves humbugs, they're her favourites." She popped the sweets into her pocket, saving them for later.

"Right then...flour and suet. Plus sugar and tea." Norman slapped each item onto the counter, keeping up a cheerful stream of chatter about characters in the town that Florence had never heard of. "Anything else?"

Florence looked longingly at the gaudily illus-trated penny dreadful books that were displayed next to the sugar mice, wishing she had remembered to bring her own few coins. In the rush of leaving it hadn't occurred to her. She fingered one that had a festive Christmas scene on the front. "Do you think you could put this by for me? This is the first year I've had enough money to buy Dulcie a Christmas present and I know she would love this."

The curtain behind the counter suddenly parted and a plump woman bustled through it, carrying sprigs of holly and ivy. "Is my Norman chatting too much?" she asked Florence, with a cheerful grin that was the spitting image of her son's. "I swear he'd forget anything and everything if I didn't remind him." She looked at the ledger where Norman had written the order down. "You must be here for Mrs Williams? From Bisley Court?"

Florence nodded. "I was just wondering if you could put this book by for my friend Dulcie?"

Mrs Crocker peered at the one she was pointing at and nodded briskly. "Tell you what...it's for your friend you say? Send her in here, and we'll give it to her ourselves. Mrs DeVere is very good supporting our business, in spite of Norman's occasional blunders." She cuffed her son good-naturedly. "Take one for yourself, and send your friend to come and get hers...and per'aps you can put in a good word with Mrs Williams so she won't be too cross with Norman."

"Oh thank you, that's so kind." Florence chose a book about the circus and put it into her basket while Norman disappeared out the back of the shop to unload a delivery.

"Between you and me, dear, my Norman isn't the brightest lad, but he makes up for it with a kind heart and hard work." Martha Crocker's eyes twinkled with amusement. "Who knows, if he meets more nice young ladies like you and your friend, he might find himself a lovely wife and make me a granny one day," she continued with a loud chuckle.

Florence laughed at the woman's admission. "I won't tell Dulcie that's your plan, but I can assure you, she is the loveliest person I know. She should have time to collect the book at twelve if she's finished with Mrs Sherringham's shopping."

She was still smiling to herself a few moments later as she strolled back along the street. She had half an hour to spare which would give her plenty of time to enjoy the colourful displays in all the shop windows. The first one she came to was a toy shop and she felt like a child again as she gazed at the myriad toys that had been artfully displayed to attract attention. Gaily painted puppets jerked on their strings, worked by the elderly owner, and there were blue-eyed dolls, tea sets, soldiers and marbles fanned out in front of him. For a moment she felt wistful at the thought of her lost childhood. The most they had been allowed at the orphanage was the occasional cast-off donated by the charitable ladies of the parish, but thankfully books were considered more appropriate and she had loved to escape into the stories they contained.

A noise further up the street caught Florence's attention and she strolled onwards to see what it was.

"Mistletoe for your sweetheart?" A street hawker was selling sprigs of mistletoe and a group of bashful young men had gathered nearby, nudging one another in the ribs.

Florence lowered her eyes, not liking the bold stares that some of them gave her and she decided to cross the road and return to the carriage across the busier market square instead.

Suddenly the air was filled with the sound of shouts and the door of the Dog and Duck tavern burst open as a cluster of men fell out onto the pavement at her feet.

"You'll pay for this, you scoundrel."

"Show me what you're made of, you cad...going behind my back like that."

Two of the men scrambled to their feet and lunged at each other again, fists flailing and their faces dark with anger. The rest of them started jeering loudly and Florence was quickly engulfed, somehow finding herself at the centre of the group.

"Want to be part of the excitement, do you, my pretty?" One of the men plucked at her shawl, slurring his words. "Come inside to the bar darlin' and I'll show you a good time." He threw his arms around her, pulling her towards the door.

"No. Get off me..." Florence tried to protest, but everyone else's attention was on the brawling men and she felt her feet slipping from under her. She was no match for his brute strength and her struggles were in vain. "Don't...please, let go of me..." The more Florence struggled, the more he laughed in her face, enveloping her in a fug of stale brandy.

Just as the drunkard was manhandling her through the door, Florence gasped as powerful hands grabbed her from behind, wrenching her from his clutches. "Leave her alone, you should be ashamed of yourself," a man's voice hissed from behind her.

"Pah...she's more trouble than she's worth." The drunkard blinked slowly and spat at the hem of her dress before stumbling back into the warmth of the tavern.

"Come with me." The man pushed her from the middle of the group of brawling, jeering men, deflecting the random blows that threatened to catch them. With one final twist, she found herself freed from the tangle of limbs and noise of cursing, standing breathlessly on the corner of a quiet side street.

Florence pushed her hair from her face, where it had unravelled from the tidy bun she had done earlier that morning. Her hands were shaking and she felt as though her heart was going to jump right out of her chest. She gazed up at her rescuer, feeling suddenly close to tears.

"You're alright, it's over now." The man's voice was warm and full of concern.

As Florence blinked, her mind cleared and she noticed the hazel eyes and knotted handkerchief at his neck. "Is it? It's you again," she exclaimed.

The man gave her a small bow. "Correct ma'am. Hunter Rudge at your service...again. Do you always get into so much trouble when you're out?" he asked, and the corner of his mouth lifted into a smile that made Florence's heart beat faster again.

She shook her head. "You have completely the wrong idea about me. It was only that one time at the Summer Fayre, and now again today. Anyone would think you made a habit of rescuing people," she added with a chuckle. "Now I'm indebted to you a second time." She smiled up at him, feeling the same pull of attraction she had felt the last time. But now it felt different...his childish features had matured and his chiselled jaw and broad shoulders made the breath catch in her throat.

Hunter Rudge peered around the corner at the men who were still fighting, scattering the passing shoppers in all directions. "They'll find out soon enough that it doesn't do to not pay attention when I'm around, especially gents as wealthy as those two." He laughed and shook his coat, making the contents of his pockets jingle.

"You're still picking pockets?" Florence rolled her eyes in exasperation. "Surely you should be on the straight and narrow by now, with a normal job? It's one thing doing it when you were a boy...but you're a grown man now."

Hunter looked at her curiously. "Why does it matter to you, Florence?" He watched the thoughts flitting across her face, like clouds scudding across the sun and felt a sudden urge to wrap her in his arms to keep her safe from all the men who wanted to do her harm.

She shrugged, not quite sure herself. "You seem like someone who wants to do the right thing, that's all. Yet you're a common thief. It doesn't make sense to me."

"Hey, less of the common, please," he said, grinning again. "I'll have you know I'm very good at this."

"That's nothing to be proud of," Florence shot back at him with a wry smile to show that she meant no harm. "You could do more, surely? An apprenticeship perhaps? Clearly, you're quick to learn."

"Maybe I didn't have any choice in the matter...a bit like you not having a choice about being in the orphanage. Did you consider that?" Hunter's face clouded. "My Pa expects me to bring in enough money to keep him happy...even though me and Ma and my younger sisters don't see much of it. Sometimes I manage to keep a bit back, just for Ma, without him knowing. She tries her best to look after the little 'uns but he has a quick temper and I worry that if I left, her life would be miserable." He lifted his hands in defeat. "It's not for lack of ambition, Florence, but sometimes it ain't as easy as you think to make a better life. I hope you don't think less of me for it?"

"Of course not, in fact I—" Before Florence could finish what she wanted to say, a voice cut across her.

"There you are...come on Hunter, we need to leave, the constables are coming." A woman in a threadbare black cloak hurried towards them. She had a panicked expression on her face as the local bobbies ran across the square to break up the fight.

"Who are you?" the woman demanded suspiciously. She pushed her hood back and rubbed her bony hands together. "I'm Celia Rudge and my husband doesn't like Hunter talking to folk like you. We keep ourselves to ourselves, don't we son." She snatched at Hunter's arm, trying to pull him away.

"Hold on Ma, she's alright. This is Florence.

Those men at the tavern were causing a ruckus and she got caught up in it."

"Your son came to my rescue," Florence explained with a reassuring smile. "If it weren't for him, I dread to think what could have happened. I was just thanking him, but I have to get back to Bisley Court now, so I'll be on my way."

The woman blinked nervously. "You're a maid at Bisley Court, are you? How...how are they all? Th...the family I mean?"

Her words came out in a stuttered rush and Hunter looked at his mother in surprise. "Why do you want to know, Ma?"

"Oh...oh, it's nothing." She waved her arm airily but Florence could tell she wanted to know. "After that fire...'twas a terrible business...I wondered whether the family got over it...I expect...I mean I hope all that money they have made up for things..." She plucked at Hunter's arm again, wincing every time she heard the constables shouting.

Florence looked at the woman in puzzlement. "I don't think money would make up for losing a child."

"No...of course not. I didn't mean that. But Mrs DeVere still has a son, doesn't she. They have someone to carry on the family line. That's what every parent want, isn't it." She gazed up at her own son with pride.

"Well I suppose so," Florence agreed.

Suddenly Celia shrank back as a thickset man with a shock of red hair came around the corner. "Oh no," she muttered hoarsely. "We need to leave Hunter, before yer pa gets angry. Did you get what we needed?"

Hunter nodded and patted his pockets. "Don't panic Ma, they won't realise they're missing a few coins until they sober up, and Florence won't tell anyone, will you?" He darted a pleading look at her, which turned to nervousness as his father bore down on them.

Florence heard the chimes of the guildhall bell ringing out over the town. "No...your secret is safe with me...I reckon I owe you a debt of gratitude for saving me from that dreadful man. I have to go anyway," she said hastily. "Mr Sawley will want to get us back to Bisley Court in case the weather turns again. Thank you for your kindness, Hunter. I'll try and keep my wits about me next time." She smiled and waved as she hurried away, wondering why Mr Rudge scowled when he heard where she was going.

"Who's that you're speaking to?" Mr Rudge's voice sounded harsh and accusatory as he steered Hunter and his mother down the nearest alley. Florence couldn't hear Celia's muttered reply but his retort was angry. "Haven't I told you never to speak to those uppity lot from Bisley Court? They're all as bad as each other."

She turned back to look, just in time to see Mr Rudge cuffing his poor wife around the ear and jabbing Hunter in the chest with enough force to send him stumbling backwards.

Hunter righted himself and put his arm protectively around his mother's shoulders as Mr Rudge stomped off ahead of them.

As Florence hurried back to the carriage, her emotions felt as though they were in turmoil. There was something about Hunter that made her pulse quicken with attraction, but she knew it would be dangerous to lose her heart to a pick-pocket. She thought about what Hunter had revealed about his father and the way she had seen with her own eyes that he ruled the family with brute force, bullying his wife and son into submission.

Who am I to judge Hunter for doing what he has to in order to keep the peace and care for his mother? How can he defy his father when that's all he's ever known. The thoughts swirled through Florence's mind as she hitched the basket higher on her arm and smoothed her hair, making herself look more presentable. She saw Dulcie helping Mrs Sherringham back into the carriage and her spirits lifted. She was excited to tell her about the gift of the penny dreadful books Mrs Crocker had promised them.

"Cooee, Florence. Did you get everything you need? Are you alright? You look a bit flustered." Dulcie grinned, pointing at the new hair ribbon Mrs Sherringham had treated her to in the haberdashery from the basket of offcuts.

"Yes, and I've got another treat to tell you about, if Mr Sawley doesn't mind stopping outside one of the shops for one minute on our way home," Florence replied. She clambered into the carriage after Dulcie, pleased to see that Mrs Sherringham was in high spirits after her successful shopping trip. The crowds of shoppers milled around the square and as the carriage lurched forwards, Florence put her hand in her pocket and touched her lucky button. She had forgotten to tell Hunter that she still had it after all these years.

Maybe I'll see him in the New Year if Mrs Moore

lets us come into town again. She hugged the thought close, hoping it would come true. Even though she knew he was thoroughly unsuitable, there was something about Hunter Rudge that made it impossible to put him out of her mind.

CHAPTER 9

⁂

The next few days passed in a whirl of activity as the servants prepared for Christmas and the guests who were coming to stay. Penelope kept up a constant stream of chatter as she trailed behind Florence doing their chores together. It made it all the more exciting as she saw the festive season through the childlike wonder of the younger girl.

"Do you think Mrs DeVere will look like a princess...will Mrs Moore let us have a mince pie after church if the vicar offers us one...will we be able to see the big tree in the drawing room once it's decorated..." Penelope's eyes widened as another thought occurred to her. "Do you think we'll have presents, Florence? I ain't never had a proper Christmas present before...imagine if I got my very own doll." She sighed with happiness, sitting back on her heels for a moment as she paused from blacking the grate in one of the guest bedrooms.

"I think the best thing is for us to press on and get our jobs done, Penelope. That way, we might be in with a chance to relax and enjoy ourselves if Mr Middleton and Mrs Moore let us." Florence stuffed a pillow into a crisply starched pillowcase and plumped it up, then smoothed the counterpane over the blankets, before standing back to make sure everything looked just how she liked it.

"Should I light the fire now?" Penelope asked. "What time are the Ellwood family arriving?"

"Yes, we need all the fires lit. Mrs Moore told me that they will be here at noon, so all the guest bedrooms need to be aired and warm in plenty of time."

Florence peered out of the window. Although the sky was dark with snow clouds, Mr Sawley had already been out in the cart earlier that morning to collect the two Christmas trees the gardener had cut from the woods. He had hurried back to tell them all that with care, the roads were passable, making Penelope giggle when he casually left a sprig of mistletoe on the dresser.

"Get away with you, Vernon Sawley," Cook had muttered, blushing furiously. "If you think I'm that easily won, you don't know me very well at all." She had shooed him back outside, but not before he had winked at Florence, protesting that it was high time Cook let someone take good care of her. "As if I have time for such shenanigans," Cook had exclaimed. Her thoughts were already turning back to the menu plan that Mrs DeVere had given her for the week that their guests would be staying and she had no time for romantic notions, no matter what Mr Sawley might be thinking.

"Tell me again who's coming?" Penelope's question reminded Florence that time was marching on and they had better start on the next bedroom. Mrs Moore was already in a bad mood and she didn't want to make it any worse.

"All I know is what Cook told me," Florence replied. "Gordon Ellwood is an old friend of Mr DeVere's. He's coming with his wife, Alyza, and their daughter Cora, I believe. We're to make up the third guest room as well in case their son joins them. He's in the 28th Regiment of Foot and there was some confusion about whether he would be back from his posting in Egypt in time for Christmas or not."

Penelope lugged the bucket of coal to the next room, puffing with exertion. "I hope I won't get tongue-tied if they ask me to do something. It's a lot to remember and I can't help but get a bit flustered sometimes, especially with people I don't know."

"Don't worry, I expect Cook will keep you busy behind the scenes. And just remember to be polite and helpful, that's what matters most." Florence gave her a reassuring grin as she got started with the lavender polish, buffing the chest of drawers until it gleamed. It felt strange that it should be her giving Penelope advice on how to be a good maid, but Florence realised that she had taken to her new role like a duck to water, and now she couldn't imagine being anywhere other than Bisley Court, with the new friends that she had made.

* * *

THE FOLLOWING MORNING, Mrs Moore summoned all the maids for an inspection in the kitchen.

"Right then everyone. Today's a very important

day and I want everything to run like clockwork, is that clear?" Mrs Moore pulled herself up to her full height and cast a critical eye over the maids assembled in front of her. "Penelope, please make sure your shoelaces are properly tied," she snapped. "We don't want another tripping over incident, do we." Her eyes took in every tiny detail until she nodded that everything was to her satisfaction.

"Come along Mrs Moore, we need to get on. They all look fine to me." Cook fidgeted, wanting to get started with the coddled eggs and ham for breakfast.

"It's all about keeping the maids disciplined, Mrs Williams. That is why you are the cook and I am the head housekeeper," Mrs Moore replied with a disparaging sniff. "The Ellwood family are important guests, and now that they're here we need to make a good impression. Please see to it that their every need is taken care of and only speak when spoken to." She gave Florence a hard look, making sure she was paying attention. "You may go about your business now."

Mrs Moore clapped her hands to chivy them on and hurried away to check that the butler had decanted the wine ready for the evening ahead. It was going to be a long day, but she was pleased they had guests staying at Bisley Court this year. It felt nice to be entertaining at Christmas again like they had when she had worked for Mr DeVere senior, before that dreadful business with the fire had cast a pall of sadness over the house.

"Good morning, Florence." Miles grinned as he passed Florence in the hallway. "Don't forget to bring me coffee later this morning. I've got a new book to show you."

"I'm going to be very busy today, Master DeVere." Florence frowned at him as Sally glided past carrying a tray of teacups.

"Of course, and I won't keep you. Papa wants to take Mr Ellwood around the estate, and Mama will entertain the ladies in her parlour I expect. Eleven o'clock should be perfect." He grinned again, once Sally was out of earshot. "Please come, Florence. You know I find it tiresome when we have people to stay. I've had an idea that I want to tell you about and you're the only person who won't laugh at me."

Florence sighed, then gave him a reluctant smile. "As long as it's quick. Mrs Moore is watching us all like hawks at the moment and Cook is like a woman possessed. She's determined the Ellwoods will tell all their friends that the food at Bisley Court is the best they've ever eaten."

Miles smiled back at her before taking his place at the dining table as Florence carried a bowl of fruit from the orangery to the sideboard. The sharp citrus scent made her mouth water and she wondered whether they might be allowed an orange too at the servants' celebratory dinner on Christmas day.

"Tell me more about how the business is going, dear fellow." Robert DeVere was in a jovial mood as he tucked into his coddled eggs and he beamed at their guests.

"It's going from strength to strength," Gordon Ellwood replied. He nodded to Sally for her to give him an extra slice of ham. "Since I've been a member of Parliament, I've been able to attract new investors and I'll be expanding my importing business next year. We'll double our tea imports and I'm thinking about going into sugar and silks as well." He shovelled a spoonful of ham and egg into his mouth and chewed it briskly.

"Having a townhouse in London has opened up so many new opportunities for us," Alyza Ellwood added. She patted Evelyn's hand. "Why don't you and Robert take a place in London...honestly

Evelyn, it's so parochial here in the West Country. Really anyone who wants to get ahead has to be in London at least some of the time, isn't that right dear?"

Gordon Ellwood nodded pompously, brushing a crumb from the tailored smoking jacket that strained over his portly frame. "Alyza's right, Robert. A man in your position shouldn't be buried away in the shires."

"Do you like being in London, Cora? I expect you'll be going to all the coming-out balls won't you?" Evelyn smiled at Cora Ellwood, encouraging her to join in the conversation. She noticed that although she had always been rather a plain child, now that she was older, Alyza ensured she wore only the finest dresses to try and make the best of her mousy brown hair and pale complexion.

"I...yes thank you Mrs DeVere. London is very nice...but I do enjoy being in the countryside best. I like going for walks and painting...that's my favourite thing to do. I mean, there's lots to paint in London too of course, but there's something about the beautiful views in the countryside that inspires me more." She blushed as Miles smiled at her, lowering her gaze to take a sip of tea.

"We're working very hard to find a suitable

match for her in London," Alyza murmured to Evelyn. "She's such a shy girl, but once she gets used to socialising, she'll come out of her shell I'm sure."

Florence glided around the table, pouring fresh tea for everyone and noticed Cora's expression fall at her mother's words. It seemed obvious to her that Cora was a country girl at heart, but her mother was having none of it.

"We're so sorry Hector couldn't join us, he would have benefited from a few days away in the country," Gordon continued. He sat back in his seat, enjoying everyone's attentive gaze. "He's doing so well in his regiment, he's tipped for promotion. They see him as a natural leader...so brave and decisive which is what they need. Of course, I shall try to persuade him to join me in the business as it expands," he added with a smug smile.

"Yes...dear Hector. I do miss him, but we're so proud of him, aren't we dear." Alyza gazed at her husband adoringly. "He takes after Gordon," she added in a loud whisper to Evelyn. "The men of the family are so marvellous, everything they do seems to work out so well."

"And what about you, Miles? I expect you're

raring to get started with following in your father's footsteps at the mill, eh?" Gordon's booming voice filled the dining room and Miles flushed as Robert's expression hardened.

"Would anyone like more tea?" Evelyn asked hastily, changing the subject before Miles could reply. "Now, let's plan our day, shall we. Chalsworth is looking very pretty so I suggest that Mr Sawley could take us for a ride out in the carriage to look at the decorations, Alyza. And you too, of course, Cora. Then we can have parlour games in front of the fire before dinner tonight. And I believe you gentlemen are going to ride around the estate?" she added, smiling at Gordon and Robert. She pushed her plate away and beckoned for Sally and Florence to clear the table. "Let's make a start. The days are so short at the moment and it looks as though the sun has come out."

"Don't worry about coming with us, Miles," Robert said flatly, giving his son a resentful stare. "No doubt you'll be too busy reading by the fire to want to come outside and hear anything Gordon and I have to talk about."

With that, everyone got up to leave, but not before Florence saw Cora give Miles a quick smile of sympathy. It seemed that they both bore the same burden of being a disappointment to their families and Florence felt a sudden rush of gratitude that Cora had shown Miles a glimmer of kindness, unlike his father.

At eleven o'clock sharp, Florence tapped on the library door, entering as soon as Miles replied.

"Thank you for coming, Florence." Miles was standing looking out of the window and Florence followed his gaze. In the distance, she could see Mr DeVere and Mr Ellwood cantering across the meadow; they made a dashing pair and she saw Mr DeVere standing up in his stirrups, sweeping his arm to point out something. The horses were kicking up snow from their hooves and crows clattered up from the bare branches in the nearby spinney, startled by the noise. Miles sighed and turned back to the desk where he had been poring over a large book. "This is what I wanted to show you." He coughed into his handkerchief and pulled his chair closer to the crackling fire.

"Are you feeling alright?" Florence gave him a concerned stare as she put the coffee and cake out for him. She had thought he'd looked better a few days ago but something about the way his breathing rattled sounded worrying. "It's so draughty in your room upstairs and this sort of weather has a way of getting into your bones if you don't move around much."

"It's nothing to worry about," Miles replied, coughing again. "Now, come and look at this book which I ordered." He pushed the heavy tome towards Florence and she came around the desk to look at it.

"Hmm...is it machinery? Something for the mill? Your father will be pleased you're taking an interest."

"No, no, no...it's not for the mill." Miles jabbed his finger impatiently at the writing under the diagram. "Look, it's a machine for making chocolate."

Florence looked again. "Chocolate? What do you want to learn about that for?" she said, stifling the urge to giggle.

Miles's face fell and she immediately felt contrite. "I'm sorry, I'm not laughing at you, I promise. It's just a bit of a surprise, that's all."

"I know...and I know you wouldn't mock my ideas, Florence because even though we haven't known each other long, I consider you to be a loyal friend."

"So why are you learning about chocolate?"

Florence bustled to the fire and added a couple of logs, before pulling a duster from her apron pocket and polishing the glass front of the bookcase. If Sally or Mrs Moore came in, it wouldn't do for them to discover her being idle.

"I've been thinking about setting up a small factory of my own. The old mill buildings at the edge of the estate are just lying empty since they moved to the new site on the far side of Chalsworth just before Papa took over."

"You mean a factory for producing chocolate?" Florence queried. "I suppose it could work, but you'd need help to get started wouldn't you? Why chocolate, instead of just working at your father's mill?"

Miles sipped his coffee and looked at Florence for a moment, as though considering whether to tell her something. "When I was a little boy and my health was bad, I used to go and sit in the kitchen. The warmth in there and the steam from the cooking seemed to help ease my lungs, so Mama didn't mind. In fact, she used to encourage it, although Papa never really knew." He flushed slightly as though embarrassed. "Cook used to let me help her and they were some of the happiest times of my life."

Florence smiled. "I can see by the look on your face that you treasure those memories. So...you'd like to do something similar...by building a factory where you can cook."

Miles nodded. "Exactly. There are large chocolate factories in the Midlands...it's nothing new." His face fell. "The only fly in the ointment is that Papa would never agree. In fact, I think he would be horrified. Can you imagine him telling his friends how proud he is of his son...who makes chocolate? Like the Ellwoods were talking about Hector's success in the regiment? I can't see it myself." Miles chuckled and shook his head, but Florence could see the hurt behind his eyes.

"You shouldn't give up on your ideas too easily, Miles." Florence paused from her dusting. "I know you want your father to approve of you, but you're eighteen...you're allowed to lead your own life."

"It's kind of you to say so, but without Papa's backing, I'd never be able to get started." His expression darkened and he suddenly stood up, throwing the rug that had been over his knees onto the floor. "Papa wants me to be more like Hector...a man who can ride and go hunting. It's this body of mine that lets me down though, Florence. If I could only show him I'm not weak, he might agree." He strode to the window and gazed out at the snowy fields again.

"You can't help your illness," Florence said hastily. She had never seen Miles like this and she wondered whether she should go and ask Cook to come and speak to him.

"My mind's made up," Miles said suddenly. "I'm going to saddle up the mare and ride out with Papa and Gordon. If I'm quick I should catch up with them soon enough."

"But...but what about your cough." Florence put her hands on her hips, feeling out of her depth. "What if it gets worse. The air is so damp...it's not good for you to be outside in it, you'll catch your death of cold."

Miles pushed past her, hurrying towards the door. "Tell Cook I won't be back until Papa and Mr Ellwood return." He seized Florence's hand, willing her to understand. "I'm fed up with him speaking to me as though I'll never amount to anything, Florence. Surely you of all people can understand that, after you told me about the matron at the orphanage saying the same about you?"

Florence nodded slowly, then grabbed the thick tweed coat that had been slung on the back of one of the chairs. "At least wear this, will you? And promise me you'll come straight back if you feel unwell." She watched with a sinking feeling as he strode off, taking the back door to get the stable block as fast as he could.

"Curse Mr DeVere and his vile comments," she muttered as she scurried off to the kitchen. "If it hadn't been for the way Hector Ellwood had been portrayed as such a success, she knew Miles would have probably stayed inside for the day. But now he was determined to prove himself. She could only hope that the dark clouds gathering over the valley might come to nothing and he wouldn't do anything reckless.

CHAPTER 10

"What do you mean, Master Miles has gone out riding?" Cook looked up from the pie lid she was brushing with milk and her eyes clouded with alarm. She darted to the door and flung it open, dashing out into the kitchen garden as though she might be able to intercept him.

"I tried to stop him, but he wasn't taking any heed of what I said." Florence shivered behind her as the first snowflakes started to fall again.

"Oh, lawks, I don't like the look of this one little bit." Cook stamped the snow off her feet and hurried back inside again. "Get the warming pans ready and put them in his bed. Hopefully, he'll come back as soon as he realises the weather's on the turn." She tipped a scoop of coal into the range and rattled the handle, making the flames leap up.

"Will he be alright? He was already coughing and I begged him not to go."

"He can be a determined young man when he wants to be," Cook replied. "Even when he was a little boy, if he set his mind to something, he would persevere until he learned it. He stuffed all those birds, you know, in the cabinet on the landing. He taught himself how to do it from books...as well as any professional. Of course, Mr DeVere didn't approve, but—" Cook bit back her words, not wanting to be accused of gossiping.

Florence busied herself in the kitchen for the next couple of hours, but the more time that passed, the more worried she felt. The snow was falling steadily now, already piling up on the windowsill and she strained her ears listening out for the sound of their return.

Suddenly there was a commotion in the hallway and the sound of running feet. Mrs DeVere had returned from their excursion into Chalsworth and she burst through the door.

"Is it true? Has Miles gone out riding on the estate? Mr Middleton just took me to one side to tell me because he's so worried." She flung back the fur-lined hood of her cape and her eyes were wide with fear.

Mrs Moore jumped up from the table where she had been checking through the menus with Cook. "I'm afraid so, ma'am. He left about two hours ago. We've banked up the fire in his room and prepared everything for his return."

Evelyn paced back and forth, wringing her hands. "I knew something like this would happen," she muttered. "Make sure you have some hot beef broth ready please, Cook." She caught sight of Florence and gave her a wan smile. "Maybe they've taken shelter in one of the old buildings; there are several dotted across the estate."

"I'm sure he'll be back any moment now with Mr DeVere," Florence replied, trying to reassure her. "He told me how much he enjoys the Christmas Eve meal...he won't want to miss that, ma'am."

"I hope you're right, Florence. I don't think I could bear it if anything happened to my boy." Evelyn sighed again.

"Perhaps it would be best if you waited in the drawing room with Mrs Ellwood and Cora," Mrs Moore said gently. "We have a warm spiced punch for you, and luncheon will be ready shortly."

"You're right." Mrs DeVere shot her a grateful smile. "Worrying won't make them come back any faster and I have our other guests to think of. Miles will be fine, he's usually such a sensible boy and knows his limitations." She hurried away with Mrs Moore, discussing the entertainments for the evening ahead.

As if on cue, the steady thrum of hoofbeats drifted through the open doorway from outside. "See, they're back already," Cook said, her face breaking into a relieved smile. "Florence, go out and meet them. Master Miles seems to listen to you more than most of us. Tell him we've put warm clothes ready for him to change into and he can have some of my special broth. He's always loved it, ever since he was a nipper."

Florence wrapped her shawl over her shoulders and dashed off through the kitchen garden towards the stables. As she rounded the corner, she saw that Mr DeVere and Mr Ellwood were in high spirits. Their cheeks were rosy from the cold and they were happily discussing business matters, without a thought for Miles who was trailing behind them.

"Oh no," Florence gasped as they got closer. The mare's flanks were slick with sweat and her ribs heaved with every breath. It looked as though they had been riding much harder than the other two men.

Tom darted out from the stable, making a beeline for Miles and his mare. "Hop off quick, Master Miles. It ain't good for her to get cold, not when she's in such a lather. If she catches a chill she'll be a goner."

"I'm so sorry, Tom, I feel terrible that she's in such a state." Miles slid wearily from the saddle, his legs almost buckling beneath him as he landed on the ground. "She got spooked by a pheasant and bolted. It was all I could manage to stay on her and stop her from getting injured. She ran through the woods and I was terrified she might impale herself on a fallen branch."

Tom grabbed the mare's reins and quickly loosened her girth. "She can be flighty, Sir. As long as I get her in the warm and give her a drink and good rub down, I think she'll be alright." The mare tossed her head, rolling her eyes fearfully as she heard a pheasant squawk in the woods. "Come on my lovely, let's get you sorted out." Tom kept up a crooning conversation, and stroked her neck, calming her instantly as he led her into the warm stable.

"You're not still making a fuss are you, Miles? For goodness sake, if you can't handle a spirited horse, you shouldn't ride out." Mr DeVere threw his reins at one of the other stable boys and slapped Gordon Ellwood on his back. "You wouldn't see Hector making such a drama about a bit of a gallop, would you?" They strolled off to get changed leaving Miles standing in the snow.

"Take no heed of him," Florence said sharply. "He's just showing off in front of Ellwood...you'd think he'd know better, but some folk speak before they think of the effects their words might have."

"So much for showing Papa what I'm made of," Miles muttered disconsolately. "When I managed to catch up with them, he seemed irritated I was there. And all they could talk about was London and who Papa should make friends with, to benefit the business." He shoved his hands in his pockets. "It's as if they're talking a different language, Florence. I'll never live up to his expectations. When the mare bolted, I thought they might come and check I was alright. But Papa just laughed and said I shouldn't have bothered coming outside."

Florence's heart squeezed with sympathy. Miles was so different from his father. Kind and sensitive, unlike Mr DeVere's bombastic manner.

She smiled up at him, determined to lift his mood. "Cook has made some broth for you, and there are warm clothes ready for you to change into. I think you should enjoy the rest of your day, regardless. Cora Ellwood seems charming...perhaps she's taken a shine to you," she added, with a mischievous grin.

Miles flushed. "Do you think?" He stared at Florence, veering between hope and despair. "Cora will have her pick of all the gentlemen of London, what on earth would she want with a feeble dullard like me."

"Stop that right now," Florence jabbed him hard with her elbow and chuckled. "You're just fishing for compliments. You know as well as I do that she blushed very prettily when you spoke to her at breakfast."

"She did ask me about the stuffed birds," Miles conceded. He looked past Florence, relieved to see that Tom was waving to let them know the mare had settled nicely. "I'd better get changed then, and—"

Before he could finish his sentence, he was seized with a bout of coughing that shook his frame.

"You need to get inside, into the warm,"

Florence said. She took his arm to steer him towards the house. "You're wet through to the skin," she added, feeling how sodden his tweed jacket was.

"I'll...be...fine in a...minute." Miles doubled over as the coughing spasms gripped him, and suddenly the snow in front of him turned crimson as he coughed up blood.

"Oh no." Florence looked on in dismay as he kicked the snow with his boot, trying to cover it up. "How long have you been coughing blood?" she demanded.

"Just the last few days," Miles replied wearily. "I didn't want to worry Mama; not with the Ellwoods coming to stay, and it being a difficult time of year for her already."

"Right, we need to sort this out right away," Florence said firmly. "I'm taking you to your room and then I'm telling Mrs DeVere. You need to see a doctor before it gets any worse, and I'm not taking no for an answer."

Miles gave her a weak smile as he leant on her arm. "As you say," he chuckled. "If this is how bossy you can be as a friend, remind me never to get in your bad books."

* * *

THE REST of the day passed in a sombre mood. Doctor Grant arrived just as the rest of the family was finishing their evening meal in the dining room, amidst a flurry of apologies that he had been delayed by a difficult case in one of the outlying villages and then his carriage had got stuck in the snow.

"Alyza, why don't you and Cora go and sit next to the fire in the drawing room," Evelyn urged. "Perhaps you could play some Christmas carols on the pianoforte, Cora? I'm sure this won't take long. I don't want to spoil the evening for you."

"We don't mind," Cora replied shyly. "We just want Miles to get well, that's what matters."

Florence hurried behind Mrs DeVere with a pitcher of hot water so the doctor could wash his hands. She was shocked to see how pale Miles looked. It was an effort for him to even lift his head from the pillows and every breath he took sounded laboured and harsh in the quiet room.

"Step outside please." The doctor waved Mrs DeVere and Florence away and they retreated to Miles's dressing room.

"Why, oh why did he go out riding?" Mrs

DeVere paced back and forth. "He should have known better, in this dreadful weather."

Florence started tidying the books on the desk, wanting to keep busy. "I...I think he wanted to show you that he's as good as..." Her words petered out as Mrs DeVere gave her a sharp look.

"As good as Hector Ellwood? Is that what you're trying to say?"

Florence swallowed and gave a small nod. "I tried to stop him, I promise."

The doctor opened the door and beckoned them both through. "The chill has gone onto his lungs...it's not looking good. He needs bed rest and nothing to upset him, is that clear. Goodness knows why he went out in the first place," he added, looking perplexed. "As I've always told you Mrs DeVere, Miles will never be a strong young man. Going out in weather like this was pure folly, it's lucky we've caught the infection now, although I can't make any promises about how this might affect him long-term." He put his jacket on again and buttoned it up.

"Isn't there anything else we can do?" Evelyn pleaded. She dabbed at her eyes with a handker-chief, trying to hold back her tears.

"We just have to wait and see." Doctor Grant

wrapped his muffler around his neck. "I'll call back in a few days, but I must get on now. I still have more people to visit...not much chance of me getting home before midnight."

After Mrs DeVere had shown him out, Florence poured some fresh water into a bowl and wrung a cloth out, pressing it gently on Miles's forehead where beads of sweat had gathered.

"I've been such a fool, Florence," Miles muttered with a wry smile. "What must you think of me, dashing after my father like some sort of lap dog, desperate for attention. And now I've spoiled Christmas for you."

Florence chuckled. "If you saw how dreadful Christmas used to be at the orphanage, you'd realise that tending to you isn't so bad. Now, you just think about that chocolate factory of yours and get better, alright?" She poured him a glass of water and held it to his lips so he could take a sip.

"You're right. It's time for me to stop feeling sorry for myself and think about the future. Thank you for giving me a different perspective, Florence."

"You might also be interested to know that Cora is most concerned about you," Florence said over her shoulder as she pulled the heavy curtains across the window to keep out the draughts.

"Don't you start matchmaking," Miles shot back with a grin.

"Would I do such a thing?" Florence giggled and shrugged innocently. "I'm just reminding you that there's plenty to look forward to when you know what to look for."

The rest of the evening passed without event and Florence yawned loudly as the clock chimed eleven. She could hardly believe how much had happened in the last twelve hours.

"I'll be up before dawn to start roasting the meat," Cook said, finishing her last cup of tea for the day.

"Why don't you get off to bed and I'll collect the glasses from the drawing room and wash them up." Florence was practically falling asleep but she knew that Cook was worried sick about Miles.

"Bless you. You're a good girl, much better than that last maid we had." Cook heaved herself to her feet and shuffled over to the range, moving the figgy pudding off the warmer where it had been simmering gently for hours.

The house was quiet as Florence let herself into the drawing room. Mrs DeVere had retired an hour ago with a headache and the Ellwoods had also turned in for an early night after complimenting Cook on a delightful meal.

"What do you want?" The deep voice came from the darkest corner of the room making Florence jump.

"Sorry, Mr DeVere. I'm just clearing up the last few things and making sure the guard is in front of the fire." Florence bobbed a curtsey and started to gather the glasses, putting them on a tray.

"I s'pose you've been pandering to that boy, have you?" Mr DeVere stumbled as he stood up from the wingbacked chair and glared at her. His words were slurred and he thrust his chin forward, looking belligerent.

"If you mean have I been tending to Miles, then yes Sir, I have. The doctor is worried about him, and—"

"Darn fool." Mr DeVere harrumphed, cutting across her words. "You have no idea, Florence. Swanning into Bisley Court, befriending Miles. Don't think I haven't noticed. It's all nothing more than a waste...all of this." He gestured vaguely with a broad sweep of his arm, almost toppling over.

"I...I'm not sure I know what you mean, Sir. I'll just check the fire and be on my way." Florence sidled past him and riddled the fire, before replacing the fireguard so no sparks could fall out onto the Persian rug during the night.

Mr DeVere sighed loudly and flopped back into his chair, muttering to himself and Florence wondered whether he had forgotten she was there. "He's such a disappointment...I wanted a strapping son to follow in my footsteps...and what have I got? A snivelling runt...all my work at the mill...all for nothing...why can't he be more like Hector...I wish we'd never lost Hugo in the fire..." He picked up his glass of brandy and emptied it in one gulp.

Florence gasped at his words. "I think that's a very cruel thing to say," she blurted out. "If you took the time to get to know Miles properly you'd see he's a kind man...with ambition too..."

"What do you mean?" Mr DeVere lumbered to his feet again and strode forward, grasping Florence's arm. "Are you telling me what I should think, about my own son? You insolent girl...how dare you." His face was dark with anger and he squeezed his hand tighter, making her wince.

"I'm sorry, Sir. I'm just tired and shouldn't have said anything. It's just that Miles is really very unwell." Florence hoped her words might placate him, but they had the opposite effect.

"I know he's unwell," Mr DeVere hissed angrily. "I don't need a lowly maid from the orphanage to tell me that." His eyes narrowed and he glared at her. "My wife never should have taken you from the mill. Mr Collier said you had ideas above your station and I can see it's true. Once Christmas is over, you will return to your position at the mill. You're a bad influence on Miles and I don't want you working here in our home."

"Oh no, please Sir. I'll try harder, I promise." Florence felt her heart sink. "Don't send me away, Mr DeVere...p...please," she begged. She couldn't believe that Mr Collier's harsh words had come true. She had ruined her opportunity for a better life and the thought of returning to the choking air of the weaving room and being separated from Dulcie brought tears to her eyes.

"Next week...you'll be gone from this house. Now get out of my way." Mr DeVere pushed her away and stumbled from the room, leaving Florence filled with despair as the hot tears coursed down her cheeks.

CHAPTER 11

*T*wo weeks later, the air was filled with the sound of gurgling water as the snow melted. Christmas felt like a distant memory and Florence's eyes were gritty with tiredness as she slipped into Miles's room with a pitcher of hot water. She didn't begrudge looking after him but between the additional work and worrying about whether he would recover, sleep had been elusive. She had managed to stay out of Mr DeVere's way for the remaining days that the Ellwoods had stayed, but yesterday he had summoned her to his study to remind her of what he had said.

Florence knew she was on borrowed time. At best she would be at the house for one more week, but she hadn't dared break the news to Dulcie yet.

Miles sat up in bed and winced as Florence opened the curtains a little to let some of the weak daylight into the room. "Must you do that?" he murmured. He tried to reach for the water but didn't have the strength to lift the glass to his mouth.

"Let me help you." Florence hurried to his side. "There's something I need to tell you," she said, as Miles closed his eyes briefly, feeling exhausted again.

His eyes fluttered open. "That sounds ominous." He smiled, but a shadow of worry clouded his eyes as he saw Florence was blinking back tears.

"I was rude to your father on Christmas Eve...he's sending me back to work at the mill." Florence tried to sound as though it was of no consequence, but the tremor in her voice gave her away.

"What? No, you can't leave. I won't allow it." Miles struggled to sit up again, looking indignant. "I shall insist to Mama that you must stay. Seeing you each day is what keeps me feeling cheerful when I'm stuck here in bed day after day."

Florence shook her head. "His mind is made up, Miles. I daren't defy him again, in case he throws me out on the street. At least I have a job and a roof over my head if I'm back at the mill."

"What did you say to him, to make him so angry?"

"He was talking about you unkindly...I didn't like it and I told him as much." Florence shrugged. "You know I sometimes speak my mind when I shouldn't."

Miles grasped her hand and squeezed it. "I don't want you to leave, Florence. You're my friend. Please will you ask Mama to come and see me? Let me try and put this right...you don't deserve to be sent away, especially not for sticking up for me."

Florence nodded but knew that it would do no good. Mr DeVere's mind was made up, and she already knew from what Cook had said during her time here that he wasn't the sort of person to have a change of heart and back down on what he had decided.

She helped Miles sit up and deftly changed the pillowcases, replacing them with freshly laundered ones that smelt faintly of lavender from the infused water that she had dabbed on them while she had been doing the ironing. The heavy book that Miles had been reading slipped to the floor and she picked it up again for him.

"A book? This is a good sign. I knew your illness must be bad when you didn't even want to read, but now it looks like you're making plans again." Florence's spirits lifted and she could see in the pale morning light that Miles's eyes looked brighter and his cheeks had lost the grey pallor they had had for the last week.

"I'm alright if I don't do anything for too long," he replied. He lifted the counterpane and pulled a sketchbook out, flipping it open. "Look, I've started jotting down a few ideas for the machines I'll need. This is the steam engine press to separate the cacao beans into cocoa butter and powder. And then I need a mould for forming the bars of chocolate."

Florence peered at his drawings and the tightly written notes on the opposite page, nodding even though she didn't understand what they were. All she cared about was the way his eyes glinted with enthusiasm as he tried to explain what each machine did. It was so different from his quiet demeanour when he talked about Thruppley Mill that knew that he would regret it if he didn't try to pursue his dream.

"This is all gobbledegook to me," Florence said with an apologetic smile. "I'll just have to take your word for it. But now I need to get on. I'll tell Mrs DeVere that you'd like to see her."

As Florence was bustling back to the kitchen, there was a loud hammering at the door and Mr Middleton creaked his way across the hall to see who had arrived with such a sense of urgency. His rheumatism didn't take kindly to the damp weather and he thought longingly of the spring days ahead.

"A letter for Mrs DeVere." The man at the door was wrapped up in a greatcoat to keep out the cold and he had a leather satchel slung across his body. "I'm to wait for her reply," he added, stepping closer to get out of the way of the melting snow that was dripping from the roof.

The butler nodded and allowed him to step inside. "Wait here please. I'll be back with Mrs DeVere's reply shortly."

Florence picked up the platter of Cook's freshly baked bread rolls and a bowl of her strawberry conserve and slipped into the dining room where Mr and Mrs DeVere were having breakfast. Mr DeVere shook his newspaper out with an irritated rustle, making Sally smirk with amusement. The maids all knew that Florence would be leaving any day and Sally had laughed spitefully when she had heard the news, telling her it was her own fault for being uppity.

Mrs DeVere broke the seal of the letter and tilted the thick paper towards the light of the lamp, scanning the contents quickly while Mr Middleton waited discreetly in the doorway.

"Well? Who's it from?" Mr DeVere sipped his tea, feeling annoyed at having his breakfast disturbed.

Evelyn read the letter again. "It's from Mrs Ellwood," she replied, looking surprised. "She's written to say how much they enjoyed their stay here at Bisley Court over Christmas."

"Quite right too. We did lay on the best of everything for them."

"But that's not all," Evelyn continued. "She says she was very sorry that Miles was so unwell. She's offering us the use of their house in Bath so that Miles can take the healing spa waters. Apparently, the doctors in London swear by it and she suggests it could be most beneficial for Miles's health."

Mr DeVere folded his paper again, giving his wife his full attention. "I suppose it couldn't harm," he said thoughtfully.

"Doctor Grant did mention it himself," Evelyn added. "But I was concerned that it might be too costly. Alyza says she would be more than happy for Miles to stay at their house for as long as he needs. They rarely use it since they're mostly in London or the Midlands."

Mr DeVere shrugged. "If Doctor Grant mentioned it, then it might be prudent. Tell Miles he has my permission to go."

"Also...Alyza has asked me whether you thought any further about Gordon's suggestion that you might take a place in London. An acquaintance of his is travelling to America for several years and their house will be left empty. Gordon suggests it would be the perfect opportunity for you to establish yourself in London society, for the benefit of getting investment for the mill."

Evelyn handed him the letter and he read it quickly. "By jove, I didn't realise Gordon was being serious when he suggested London. But you know what...I think this could be just what we need. He can introduce me to his contacts. It can only be a good thing for the business. In fact, I think I should go up right away; I don't want to miss out." He drained his cup and stood up. "I'll write a letter back to Gordon Ellwood telling him I'll be there in a couple of days. Collier can take care of the mill in my absence."

Evelyn nodded, standing up too. "I'll accept Alyza's kind offer of the house at Bath too. I can stay with Miles to start with, and then if you'd like me to join you in London for a while to accompany you to social events and entertain your new contacts, it's simple enough for me to come up." She hurried off to her parlour, leaving Florence and Sally to clear the table.

"Miles will forget all about you, soon enough," Sally whispered as she stacked the dishes. "He'll be settling into a new life in Bath, and you'll be back where you belong, scuttling underneath the weaving looms like a cockroach." She chuckled as Florence swept up the crumbs on the tablecloth, trying to ignore her jibes.

It's true. Miles might see me as a friend, but Cook was right...we're always just workers to make their life easier at the end of the day. Florence's heart felt heavy as the thoughts rattled through her mind. She was glad that Miles was getting the chance to improve his health, but she would miss him. She knew that once she returned to the mill, she would probably never see him again.

She spent the rest of the day in the kitchen,

helping Cook prepare all of Miles's favourite foods for him to take. "I know Mrs Ellwood said her housekeeper at Bath is a decent cook, but she won't know what Master Miles likes, will she?" Her cheeks wobbled with indignation at the thought of someone else taking care of Miles. "What if he takes a turn for the worse again? I doubt very much if her beef broth will be as good as mine."

Florence shot her a sympathetic smile. "I don't think he'll be away for very long, Cook. From what Mrs DeVere said, it might just be a couple of months."

Cook pushed her sleeves up and tipped a pound of dried fruit into the cake batter she was mixing while shaking her head gloomily. "He's only eaten my food for as long as I can remember, Florence. It just won't be the same with him gone..." Her eyes misted over and she blinked furiously.

"I'll miss him too," Florence said quietly. "Will you write to me...when I'm back at the mill. I'd like to know that he's better."

Cook nodded. "I wish you were staying here with us, Florence. You need to learn to think before you speak. You're one of the best maids we've ever had...it's a terrible waste, just when you were doing so well."

Suddenly there was a rustle of silk and Mrs DeVere swept into the kitchen.

"Good morning ma'am, I'm making good progress with the food for Miles." Cook stirred the cake mix even faster. "Do you think he would like some of my chocolate fancies to take as well? He used to love helping me make those when he was a little boy."

"Oh, whatever you think best Mrs Williams. Don't forget we will have a cook there to take care of us in Bath. Not that her food will be a scratch on yours, of course," Mrs DeVere added hastily.

Florence turned back to the apples that she was peeling ready for making a fruit pie, not wanting to meet her eye. Even though she stood by what she had said to Mr DeVere that fateful night in the drawing room, she felt a sense of guilt that somehow she had let the family down. Mrs DeVere had wanted to give her a chance, but her own hot-headedness had ruined it.

"Actually it was Florence who I want to see."

Florence looked up in surprise. "Me ma'am?" Her mouth went dry and her mind whirled, wondering what else she might have done to incur

Mr DeVere's disapproval. Perhaps he had told his wife that she was to leave immediately now that Miles would no longer need her.

"I've just come from speaking with Miles. He is quite insistent that you should accompany us to Bath for the time he's taking the spa waters."

"But...but what about Mr DeVere's orders ma'am. He wants me to return to Thruppley Mill." Florence felt a flush of gratitude that Miles had been true to his word, even though she knew it wouldn't have any bearing on what Mr DeVere wanted.

"Don't worry about that." Evelyn DeVere suddenly smiled and for a moment, it was as if all the worries of the last few weeks had melted away. She was a very beautiful woman, but all too often her good looks were marred by sadness.

"I have spoken to Mr DeVere and...with a little gentle persuasion, he had come around to my way of thinking. In spite of his illness, Miles has seemed much happier since you have been looking after him. So you will come with us to Bath, and afterwards, your place back here at Bisley Court is secure."

"Oh, thank you Mrs DeVere. I really do promise to do better. I didn't mean to be rude to

Mr DeVere...I just wanted him to see Miles as the kind person he is." Florence clapped her hand to her mouth as Cook darted her a warning look for speaking too frankly again. "S...sorry Mrs DeVere...I'm very grateful and I'll do whatever I can to help Master Miles get better again."

Evelyn DeVere coughed discreetly into her handkerchief to hide a smile of amusement. "Just remember that Mr DeVere is the head of the household, Florence. You don't need to fight Miles's battles...but you're right...even though he's not physically strong, Miles will make a success of his life somehow, because he's a very determined young man."

Florence nodded happily and started peeling the apples faster than ever. She felt as though she might cry with joy that her future at Bisley Court was safe. It was all she had wished for since her argument with Mr DeVere and she had Miles to thank for it.

"We leave the day after tomorrow," Mrs DeVere added. "We'll be away for a couple of months I expect, so please pack Master Miles's clothes accordingly."

* * *

"Giddyup." Vernon Sawley flicked the reins over the horses and the carriage rumbled down the driveway, throwing up slush from the wheels.

"Are you sure you're warm enough?" Florence asked again, reaching for another rug.

Miles grinned at her. "Dulcie, will you please tell her to stop fussing. I'm not a complete invalid."

Dulcie giggled and jabbed Florence with her elbow. "Master DeVere needs peace and quiet, not you wittering on like a mother hen."

"Alright, maybe I am fussing...just a little," Florence conceded. "I just want to make sure everything goes without a hitch now that I've been given a second chance."

"Papa will be away in London quite a lot from now on I imagine, so there's no need to worry." Miles sat back in the carriage and smiled to himself. Florence didn't need to know that he had told his mama he doubted whether he could even conceive of the idea of taking the spa waters while he felt so bad about Florence being sent away on his account. Evelyn had looked most alarmed at the thought of losing out on Mrs Ellwood's kind offer and had hurried off to persuade his papa, just as he had hoped.

"So tell me what the plan is again? I've never

been anywhere as grand as Bath. You'll have to tell me all about it when you get back." Dulcie had felt a moment of envy when she heard the news, but once Florence had explained how close she had come to being sent back to the mill, she was relieved for her friend.

"Mr Sawley is going to take us to Chalsworth train station, and we'll get the train to Bath. Mrs DeVere is joining us tomorrow. And then you'll be starting at the spa next week, is that right Master Miles?"

Miles nodded absentmindedly. He was already thinking about how he might be able to spend more time on his plans to make chocolate bars once his health returned. He watched the fields slipping past outside and pondered who he might like to sell his chocolate to. His initial thoughts were leaning towards a recipe that might appeal to the wealthier customers because he knew that his father would find that more compelling when the time came to reveal his plans. He allowed himself a moment to daydream about supplying the finest dining establishments in London...perhaps even to the royal family.

"It's lucky Mr Sawley had room for me today," Dulcie replied. Mrs Sherringham has decided it's time for her to start coming out of mourning. She's asked me to order her a new shawl with a coloured trim. Nothing too gaudy, of course. But perhaps a nice soft purple or dark red."

"You seem well settled there, Dulcie. Do you like it?" Florence had noticed that Dulcie was blossoming in her new position and she felt happy for her. "I'll miss you while we're away, but I hear there are some lovely haberdashery shops in Bath so I'll try and buy you a new hair ribbon, or a little something."

"I really do," Dulcie said with a smile. "Mrs Sherringham is a very considerate mistress to work for. She told me I have a very good eye for colour; that's why she wants the new shawl because I suggested it would suit her, without being disrespectful to Mr Sherringham's passing. She's even going to let me start taking dressmaking lessons. She said it would be good to improve myself."

Florence grinned at her. "Dulcie Pickering, I scarcely recognise you anymore. So much for Matron saying we'd never come to anything, eh? If she could see us now..."

As the carriage rumbled over the cobbled streets of Chalsworth, Florence tied her shawl tightly around her shoulders. "I won't be long, Miles. Mrs DeVere asked me to purchase some menthol-ease and cherry cough syrup from the pharmacy to take with us. I'll be back as soon as I can."

"And I only have to go to the dressmakers and Mrs Crocker's grocery store," Dulcie added. "Mr Sawley will take me back to Bisley Court once we've taken you both to the station."

"There's no rush. The train doesn't leave for a little while." Miles was grateful to have a few moments to rest by himself in the peace of their carriage before the train journey. He still felt exhausted, but he didn't want to make a fuss.

Florence smiled to herself as she watched Dulcie hurrying towards the grocery store. Dulcie had mentioned Norman Crocker several times in recent weeks, remarking how much she had enjoyed the book Mrs Crocker had given them, and each time her cheeks had coloured. She tried to imagine Dulcie happily married to someone like Norman and found she liked the idea.

"I hope Master DeVere is feeling a bit better now?" The tall pharmacist peered over the top of his glasses as he handed Florence her purchases. "Doctor Grant told me that a visit to Bath Spa was on the books...after all these years of ill health, it would be wonderful for Master DeVere to be cured once and for all."

Florence nodded and counted out the coins that Mrs DeVere had given her. "We're all wishing for a cure and Master DeVere has high hopes that he'll make a recovery." She let herself out of the shop and glanced up the street. Dulcie had just turned into the dressmakers where she knew she would be for at least ten minutes. She put her hand in her other pocket and pulled out a couple of coins, coming to a decision.

"A notebook, you say?" The shopkeeper in Chalsworth's only bookshop paused from dusting the leather spines of the books in front of him.

"Yes please, Sir. I only have a shilling and sixpence though. Do you have one that I can afford?"

The shopkeeper scratched his head then rummaged in a box under the counter. "Will this do?" He pushed the book towards her. It had a smart red cover and there was a gold stripe on the spine. "It's normally two shillings but I can let you have it for less, just this once."

Florence hesitated then handed over the money. She doubted that was the real price, but she knew there was no point trying to beat him down. "Thank you, that will do nicely." She tucked the notebook in her basket and hurried back along the street, hoping that Miles would like his gift.

"You're in a tearing hurry. Don't tell me you're in trouble again?"

The deep voice from the alleyway stopped Florence in her tracks and she span around, to find herself face to face with Hunter Rudge.

"Not this time. There's no need to save me from any mishaps today," she chuckled. Her heart skipped a beat as he lifted his cap and gave her a small bow. His tousled dark blonde hair flopped over his brow and his hazel eyes glinted with amusement.

"It's nice to see you in town again." Hunter swung the sack that he had over his shoulder onto the ground where it landed with a thud.

"What on earth is in that?" Florence frowned hoping it wasn't what she thought. "Don't tell me you've moved onto stealing bigger things. Honestly, Hunter...I wish you would take care. If the constables catch you, you'll get thrown into prison and what hope would I have of seeing you then?" She blushed as she realised how forward that sounded. "Not that you've been on my mind," she added hastily.

Hunter threw back his head and laughed. "Give me the benefit of the doubt, Florence. I'm not all bad." He opened the sack and pointed at the jumble of tools inside. "I fix a few things for people, that's all. You'd be surprised how many of the shop-keepers need someone handy and I've always been good at mending things, out of necessity."

Florence raised one eyebrow, wondering whether he was being entirely truthful. "With what I know about you, it looks more like you might be breaking into the shops, not fixing things for them." She wished she could have bitten her words back as she saw the shadow of hurt cross his face. "Sorry, that was unkind of me. I know you're just trying to do your best."

Hunter shrugged and grinned at her again, his good humour restored. "I thought about what you said last time. I still have to do a bit of the pick-pocketing, to keep Pa happy, but only ever from those who I think can spare it. The wealthy folk who let their guard down after a few too many drinks in the tavern. But doing these mending jobs adds a few more coins to the coffers each week.

Who knows, one day I might be completely on the straight and narrow," he added with a chuckle.

The town hall clock chimed and Florence saw Dulcie heading towards the carriage. "I won't see you for a little while. I'm going with Master DeVere to Bath, so he can take the waters. He's been terribly unwell." She turned to go and wished they could talk for longer.

"I'll still be here," Hunter replied casually, lifting his cap again. He swung the sack back over his shoulder and watched Florence walking away.

As the carriage bowled past a few moments later, Hunter stood in the shadows watching curiously. He had never seen Miles DeVere, although just like most people in Chalsworth, he knew of him. He saw that Florence was laughing at something Miles had said, her face glowing with happiness, and felt a pang of something he couldn't quite put his finger on. Jealousy...regret...he wasn't sure but it left him feeling flat.

He sighed and continued on his way. It was no use wishing he might be able to make Florence laugh like that one day, even though he longed to. She lived in a different world from him, and by the look of things, Miles DeVere seemed to have taken quite a shine to her. Although she was friendly towards him, Hunter knew he could never offer her more than a life where they would always be waiting for the constable's knock at the door, or scraping to get by. He hurried onwards to his next job, telling himself that after everything she'd already been through at the orphanage and Thruppley Mill, she deserved better than that.

CHAPTER 12

Florence flicked the curtains open and paused for a moment to take in the view. The elegant sweep of honey-coloured houses in the crescent on the opposite side of the narrow park had a pleasing symmetry, with smart iron railings along the front, and steps leading to the tall front doors. She could see that even though it was barely daybreak, there were already several servants busily scrubbing the front steps and the barrow boys were making their way along the cobbles to sell their fresh fruit and vegetables.

"Time to get up Master Miles. You have an early appointment today if you recall." She knelt down and briskly shovelled the ash from beneath the grate in the hearth into the awaiting bucket, before adding some fresh coal and squeezing the bellows. The new flames leapt up, quickly taking the chill off the room.

"Are you taking me or is Mama coming?" Miles sat up in bed. His hair was sticking up at all angles and he rubbed the sleep from his eyes.

"Mrs DeVere has asked me to take you today." Florence poured hot water into the bowl on the washstand and dunked a cloth into it, wringing it out and handing it to Miles with a smile. "She's going to be busy today going through the menu with Mildred. Mrs Ellwood and Cora will be here in a few days and she wants to make sure they have a nice time."

Miles scrubbed the hot cloth over his face and smoothed his hair down, before swinging his legs out of the bed. His nightclothes did little to hide how thin he had become and he sighed with frustration as Florence passed him the crutches that he now used to get around.

"Don't be impatient with yourself," Florence said quietly. She knew how much he hated feeling so weak.

"It's been almost four months already, Florence. I thought I'd be all better and back home at Bisley Court again by now." Miles shuffled slowly to the window and looked out, watching the costermongers wheeling their barrows past on the street below. "I'd give anything to be as strong as them," he muttered.

"Give it time, Miles. You said the doctors were pleased with your progress when you met with them last week. I think you underestimate just how ill you were over Christmas." Florence draped his clothes on the rack in front of the fire to warm them up ready for him to get dressed.

"How do you manage to always see the good in any situation?" Miles raised an eyebrow and shook his head with a chuckle. "Most days I like you being so happy, but some days...well, you're determined not to let me wallow in self-pity, even if I want to."

"That won't do you any good, will it," Florence shot back. She picked up the ash bucket and turned to leave. "You have to look at what's good in your life, Miles. Besides...Cora won't want to spend time with you if you're grumbling about not getting well as fast as you'd hoped, will she?" She grinned and darted away as he rolled his eyes.

Even though it was only the end of April, there was a real sense of warmth in the air as Florence wheeled Miles in his bath chair through the quiet back streets of the city. At first, he had been determined not to use a bath chair, claiming with exasperation that they were only for the elderly, but his doctors had insisted, telling him that the weakness in his lungs had compromised his whole body, hence why he found walking so tiring.

"Are you taking in the fresh air?" Florence reminded him as they walked along the outskirts of the park. The avenue of trees that lined the edge of the park had already unfurled their acid green leaves, and the breeze sent a flurry of pink and white blossom swirling over them like snowflakes.

"There's no peace with you, is there?" Miles sat up straighter and took several deep breaths. His spirits lifted as he realised that he could now go for a few minutes without succumbing to a coughing fit. It was a small improvement but noticeable nonetheless.

"You see...you couldn't do that a few weeks ago," Florence said triumphantly from where she steered the bath chair behind his head.

Once she had helped Miles out of the bath chair and seen him safely to the room where his physician would give him hydrotherapy treatment in the hot spring waters, Florence was free to do as she pleased for the next hour. Compared to the busy days at Bisley Court where a steady procession of chores filled every waking moment from dawn until dusk, taking Miles to his appointments at the spa made a welcome change. She made a point of getting up early to get all her jobs in the house done before they left so that occasionally she had a rare morning off to explore the city if Mrs DeVere didn't need her to race back to the house to do anything.

"Good morning miss, penny for a cup of coffee." The perky voice of the coffee seller at the corner of the street caught her attention and she nodded, handing over a coin.

"Very tasty, as per usual, Fred. I hope your ma and the nippers are keeping well." She sipped gratefully at the drink, watching everyone going about their business. The clerks hurried past, black coats flapping like crows shaking out their wings in the breeze, intent on getting behind their desks as quickly as possible. She noticed that many of them wore spectacles, with poor eyesight from peering at ledgers all day in gloomy lamplight.

Horses clopped past pulling smart carriages along the street bearing well-dressed ladies to the shops where they would stroll, admiring the window displays. Florence wondered idly what it must be like to lead such a life of leisure where you weren't at anybody's beck and call.

Come along girl, remember what life was like in the mill. This is like heaven compared to those times. The thought brought a smile to her face, reminding her she had a lot to be grateful for and she gulped down the rest of her coffee, handing her tin cup back. "Thank you, Fred. Tell me, how long does it take to walk to the new emporium from here?"

The boy on the coffee stall gave her a gap-toothed grin. Unlike most of the people he served, Florence took the time to ask after his family, so he always gave her a bit more coffee than most people in her cup. "About ten minutes if you cut through via St Giles's churchyard and don't hang around," he replied, pointing down the street to a narrow alleyway.

A few minutes later, Florence slid through the creaky wooden gate at the end of the alleyway and found herself at the far corner of the churchyard where the spaces between the graves were over-grown and there was an air of neglect. Many of the headstones listed slightly and were covered in yellowing lichen. She pushed through the long grass heading for the gravelled pathway that would take her directly to the next street. A robin hopped ahead of her, tilting its head to look at her with its button black eyes. It felt quiet away from the bustle of the road she had just left but she could see the vicar speaking to one of his parishioners by the heavy church door. The gardener who was clipping the yew hedge next to the vestry gave her a polite nod and she felt reassured that it was safe to be taking the shortcut. She patted her pocket to check that the coins were still there. She had been saving up from her weekly pay and wondered what Dulcie would most like as the gift she had promised to bring back for her.

Suddenly she heard the sound of running feet crunching on the gravel behind her and she twisted around to see what the commotion was.

"Grab 'er...get the money." A scruffy urchin lunged forwards, thrusting a hand into her dress pocket, while his friend kicked the back of her legs, making her crumple to the ground. She gasped as her head hit the edge of a gravestone with a dull thud.

"Hey...get off me, you little..." Florence tried to grab the boy, but he was as slippery as an eel, wriggling from her grasp.

"Serve you right for comin' through the churchyard..." The boy leered at her and darted forward again, snatching the tortoiseshell comb from out of her hair.

"Get out of here, you little tinkers," a voice boomed, sending the boys scampering away. Florence sat up feeling dazed. "Are you alright?" The kindly face of the vicar swam into view and she nodded, not trusting herself to speak.

"It's my own fault, I should have known better than to come this way." Florence took the vicar's arm as he helped her stand up. She pushed her hair back from her face and felt in her pockets. To her dismay, not only had her money gone, but the lucky button that Hunter had given her all those years ago had been taken too. She blinked back her tears.

"Here, let's get you to a seat where you can catch your breath." The vicar steered her to the nearest bench, handing Florence his handkerchief so she could dry her eyes. She perched on the edge of the bench, feeling suddenly shaky with delayed shock.

"We're not normally bothered by pick-pockets here...most of them know better because my dear wife tries to help them out with any food we can spare, so there's a certain level of respect, I suppose." He shook his head with a kindly smile. "I know exactly who those two boys are and I'll be having a stern word next time I see them, you can rest assured of that."

"I'm alright, it was just a bit of a nasty surprise that's all. They took my lucky charm...it's given me hope even in the darkest times and it was very special because someone I admire gave it to me."

"Oh, dear. That's even more disappointing."

"And I wanted to buy my friend Dulcie a present...but I'll have to wait until I've saved up a few more coins now." She gave the vicar a shaky smile. "If you could walk me back to the street, I'd be most grateful. I have to get back to the spa where my master is taking the waters. I can't be late getting back."

The vicar nodded and tucked her hand into the crook of his arm. "Do you go to church?" he enquired mildly as they walked slowly towards the lych gate.

Florence flushed. "I do when I can, vicar. But since we're only staying in Bath for a while, I confess I have been lax."

He patted her hand gently. "Stay close to the Lord, my dear. When you are troubled, He will always listen to you, and when you are grateful for good things, give thanks to Him. You don't need a lucky charm to have good fortune in your life...just do your best and see what unfolds."

Florence felt comforted by his words as she returned to collect Miles. She had attached too much significance to the gift from Hunter, and she smiled to herself at the irony that he had probably stolen the button in the first place, from an unsuspecting onlooker at the Summer Fayre. As for Dulcie's present, it looked like they would be staying in Bath for at least another month so she would ask Mrs DeVere if she could go to the emporium another day and get her a pretty hair ribbon once she'd managed to save up a few more pennies.

* * *

"You're looking much better Miles, I'm very glad to see." Alyza Ellwood sipped daintily on her sherry as she observed Miles. "It was Cora's idea to suggest you should come to Bath and take the waters, you know. Of course, as soon as she said it, I knew it would be perfect."

Miles raised his glass and smiled at Cora. "In that case, my heartfelt thanks for such a splendid suggestion."

"I have to agree," Evelyn DeVere added. "I know we have some way to go, but the doctors have told us that although Miles might always have to be careful in the winter months, the damage his lungs sustained as a baby need not affect him forever. It really has been a revelation, and we've most grateful for your generosity, Alyza."

Florence hovered discreetly next to the table, serving each person with the delicious beef casserole that Mildred had been cooking since early that morning. Her mouth watered as the meaty aromas filled the room.

"How is your coming-out season progressing, Cora? I expect you're having so much fun choosing your gowns and attending all the soirees in London." Evelyn noticed that Cora had become more confident since she had visited Bisley Court at Christmas. Clearly being in London was having the effect Alyza had hoped it would.

"It's very nice, thank you Mrs DeVere, although I must confess I sometimes long for a quiet week. I miss being able to paint, but Mama says all my efforts have to be focused on meeting the right people."

"Well, quite, my dear. You'll never meet a suitable husband shut away in the parlour dabbling with paints, will you?" Alyza tucked into her casserole, not noticing the brief smile that passed between Miles and her daughter.

"Did you bring your paints with you to Bath?" Miles asked. "The doctors tell me I have to spend at least an hour outside every day in my bath chair. Perhaps I could accompany you to the park. The gardens are delightful and there's a very pretty view of the river and the bridge. Florence and I noticed some other artists painting there recently."

Cora blushed. "I...I wouldn't call myself an artist, but if Mama agrees, that would be wonderful. The spring blossom against the river would be perfect for a watercolour painting."

Evelyn DeVere gave her son a curious look and took a sip of wine to hide her smile. It seemed that it wasn't only the mineral waters at the spa that were lifting his spirits.

"It looks as though this fine weather is set to last for the next few days. Why don't I ask Mildred to pack a picnic and you can go tomorrow?" She glanced at Cora, pleased to see that her face had lit up at her idea. "Alyza, I don't want to be presumptuous, but would you accompany me to the new department store? There are five floors and everyone in Bath is talking about it. I thought we could go together, and then tomorrow evening, I wondered if we could all go to the theatre."

"The department store sounds like a wonderful idea for the two of us," Alyza replied. "If your maid Florence accompanies Miles and Cora, I don't think it would be considered improper for them to go the park without us chaperoning them. It's so long since we came to Bath, I've quite forgotten what a beautiful city it is, especially after the smog we've had to endure in London this winter."

The rest of the day passed in a whirlwind of activity in the kitchen for Florence. Mildred was determined to prove her cooking skills were every bit as good as the cook the Ellwoods used in London, and by the end of the day, there were platters of freshly made pies and cakes, with enough food to feed everyone three times over. "I used to wish they'd taken me with them to London," Mildred confided. "It was so quiet here, but my old Ma begged Mrs Ellwood to let me stay here so I could look after her since my Pa died. Mrs Ellwood was very good to agree, but it has been nice seeing the house full again."

Florence draped a muslin cloth over the cakes

as they cooled. "They seem like a nice family, especially Cora."

"Oh, yes, Miss Cora is such a poppet," Mildred said fondly. "She used to love coming in the kitchen when they stayed here when she was a little girl. I used to lift her onto the stool and she wanted to have a go at stirring everything."

Florence nodded thoughtfully, thinking back to the way Miles had described escaping into the kitchen as a little boy. It was almost as though Miles and Cora were made for each other.

The following day dawned fair and there was a palpable air of excitement in the house. Mildred had already packed the picnic food into a sturdy basket and dug out a large woollen blanket from the back of the linen cupboard for them to sit on.

"You look charming, I must say." Miles bowed slightly as Cora came down the stairs in a sprigged cotton gown in pale blue, topped by a dark blue velvet cloak in case it was chilly next to the river. She had a satchel over her shoulder and carried a small portable easel.

"Thank you, that's very kind of you." Cora flushed as she checked she had everything she needed and Florence was glad to see that she wasn't flirting coquettishly with Miles. The last thing she wanted was for Miles to have his heart broken by someone who might play him for a fool.

Florence pushed the bath chair along the wide pavements, taking care to avoid the rough cobbles where possible. Cora walked alongside the bath chair, pointing out landmarks to Miles and before long they had settled for a sheltered spot next to a large willow tree that gave them a good view of the sweeping river and elegant buildings beyond.

"You might say you're not an artist, but I beg to differ." Miles leaned on his crutches admiring the watercolour painting which had quickly come to life on Cora's canvas. She had confidently washed the colour on, building each layer up, and after a couple of hours had created a charming likeness of the colourful flowerbeds in front of the river and crescent of buildings beyond.

"Just a tiny bit more pink for the blossom and then I'll be finished." Cora dabbed her brush with a flourish and turned to Miles with a broad smile. "Thank you so much for suggesting this; it's been the best day I've had for ages."

"Shall I serve the picnic now?" Florence spread the rug out and lifted out the pies and cakes.

"Thank you, Florence, and please join us. If it

weren't for you, I'd be stuck inside most days." He grinned at Cora. "Florence keeps me on the straight and narrow, making sure I do everything the doctors tell me to do. I should be strong enough to start putting my ideas into action when I go back to Bisley Court, thanks to Florence's nagging," he added with a chuckle.

Over lunch, Miles spoke about his ideas for the chocolate factory while Cora listened attentively. "What I really want to do is have a business where the workers are well taken care of. Papa says that I'm hopelessly liberal and that the workers would become idle and entitled..." he shrugged, suddenly looking bashful. "Perhaps he's right. He's been very successful with the mill, after all. And I just have a head full of ideas...or daydreams."

"I think it sounds like a noble ambition," Cora declared stoutly. "My own Papa sometimes talks about the bills of reformation for people in factories in Parliament, but some of the poor wretches I see in London look like they'll never get out of poverty. You could play a part with your ideas. Reform has to start somewhere."

"It seems we're of a similar mind," Miles replied, smiling happily. "Florence is the only person I've confided in until now. I don't think Papa will approve of my ideas at all."

"If he spends as much time in London as my Papa...perhaps you could make a start without him finding out?" Cora's eyes sparkled with intrigue. "If you show you're committed, he might be more inclined to take your plan seriously."

"Well, now that you're privy to my plans, you and your mother will have to come and visit us again when we're back at Bisley Court, so you can see my progress, as long as you keep it secret for now," Miles replied. His face clouded slightly. "As long as it doesn't interfere with your London season, of course. Who knows, you might be engaged to marry the next time we meet."

As Florence pushed Miles back to the house in the late afternoon sun, her thoughts turned unexpectedly to Hunter Rudge. Seeing Miles and Cora speaking with such animation about the future had given her a pang of envy at their easy camaraderie. Although she had only met Hunter a few times, she had felt a spark of connection with him that was hard to explain...one that felt as though they could be easy in each other's company. But she also knew there could be no future in it. Just as Cora was following a path that would most likely lead her away from Miles, with marriage to a suitable man in London, Hunter's criminal ways meant that their friendship could never come to anything either.

"Not far now," she said, lifting her chin as they rounded the corner on their way home. She decided there was no point pining over what couldn't be. For now, there was another month in Bath to enjoy, and once she was busy back at Bisley Court she would just have to put Hunter Rudge out of her mind and concentrate on making the most of life serving the DeVere family instead.

CHAPTER 13

A sharp wind whistled down the valley, rattling the last few withered leaves from the trees in the spinney and Florence tightened her shawl. The path she followed was well worn, taking her across the manicured lawns of Bisley Court, then winding through the scrubby grassland and woods beyond until it joined the river for the last stretch of her journey. Jasper, Miles's glossy yellow labrador lolloped along behind her, darting into the bushes every time he heard a rustle in the undergrowth.

"Come on silly, you're far too noisy to catch a rabbit, they're long gone." Florence scratched his ears as he gambolled back to walk by her side. She lifted the basket higher on her arm and his ears pricked up. "Yes, I'm sure Miles will give you a nice bit of pastry from his pie," she chuckled.

As she rounded the corner in the last part of her walk, the trees gave way to a wide clearing where the old mill building sat in the low winter sunshine. Every time she saw it, she marvelled that old Mr DeVere's business has started from such humble beginnings. Compared to the sprawl of buildings at Thruppley Mill now, this was just a simple stone building but it was perfect for what Miles had in mind.

"Go on then, go and find him." Florence pointed to the open door and Jasper bounded up the steps ahead of her. "I've brought some food for you," she called.

Miles levered himself out of the chair where he had been sitting, tinkering with the machine in front of him. "Good timing, I was just starting to get hungry." He brushed his hair off his forehead, leaving a smudge of dirt.

"Are you sure you're going to have this up and running in time for when your father gets back for Christmas?" Florence cast a dubious look at what seemed to be a rusty pile of items that were only fit for the rag and bone man to take away for a few pennies.

"Have faith, Florence. It's all coming together." Miles patted the metal panel in front of him as though it was an animal, sending a cloud of dust from its bowels onto the wooden floorboards below and making them both cough.

"Well eat this quickly, while it's still warm." Florence wiped the chair with the corner of her apron and opened the basket, releasing the smell of pheasant pie.

They sat in companionable silence for a moment, savouring the buttery pastry while Jasper sat in front of them drooling slightly as he watched each mouthful with a hopeful glint in his eye.

"I can still hardly believe the change in this place since we got back from Bath...you've achieved so much, and in just a year and a half too." Florence looked around, remembering the first time Miles had asked her to wheel him down here. It had taken a good hour to manoeuvre the bath chair over the rough ground but with a bit of effort and determination, plus hacking away at the brambles which had given Florence blisters that lasted days, they had made it there.

Back then, the building had been scarcely visible in the landscape. Ivy had grown up every wall, threading its tendrils in through the windows, and the main door sagged off its hinges. She had helped Miles up the steps, shouldering the door open with a deafening screech of wood on stone and then he had shuffled around on his crutches to assess what state it was in. Pigeons had flapped indignantly above their heads, at the sudden intrusion of their domain and Florence jumped when she saw rats scuttling away. The building had seemed like a lost cause to Florence's untrained eye and she wondered whether it would be an impossible feat to get it habitable again. But for once, Miles had been the one to see the positive side of things. He had been bubbling with excitement, already seeing the small factory in his mind's eye, with machines humming busily and the sun slanting through the windows.

Jasper gave a small whine, looking longingly at their picnic lunch and bringing Florence back to the present.

"The main thing was that the roof was sound," Miles mumbled through a mouthful of food. "Without that, the timbers would have rotted and it would have been much harder to rescue the place."

Florence riddled the coals in the stove in the corner of the room and put the kettle on the hot plate to boil. "Are you sure this old thing is keeping you warm enough?" she asked. She added a scoop of tea leaves to the sturdy brown teapot as the kettle began to whistle and poured the boiling water in. "It feels terribly draughty in here to me and you're not moving around much to keep warm." She handed Miles a cup of tea and opened up the basket again for the dark fruitcake that Cook had popped in there for them.

"I can't afford to stop now. I want to get as much done as I can to surprise Papa when he comes back from London—"

"But not at the expense of your health," Florence countered hastily. "I heard you coughing as I was coming up the steps. It's not just yourself that you have to think about now. Cora would be so upset if you got ill again."

Miles smiled ruefully. "There you go again, like an old mother hen. Anyone would think you were a granny instead of an eighteen year old girl." He drained the rest of his tea and stood up slowly, using two sticks to steady himself. "You worry too much Florence. I won't do anything to jeopardise my wedding in the summer. Cora is far too precious to me, to do that."

"I should think so. You don't want to end up

back in Bath at the spa, recuperating for months again."

"Well, Cora sent me a letter to say they will be coming here for Christmas as Mama has invited them. I want her to be proud of what I've achieved, as well as Papa."

Florence re-packed the basket with the dirty plates to take back to the kitchen and threw a crust on the floor for Jasper which he wolfed down eagerly.

"Cora adores you for who you are. Just like I told you last year when you were dithering around, hoping she might notice that you loved her."

Miles shot her an amused look as he resumed his work. "I'm still a bit shocked that she said yes to my proposal if I'm honest. You know I only hesitated because I didn't think it was fair to expect her to tie herself to an invalid like me when she had the pick of all those eligible bachelors in London."

"Mrs Ellwood might have thought they were eligible, but it was as plain as the nose on my face that Cora never wanted a high society life in the city. She's a country girl through and through." Florence whistled for Jasper. "As for tying herself to an invalid...maybe you should take heed of what I said. It's freezing in here and you don't want to get ill again this winter."

She rolled her eyes as Miles waved her concerns away and started hammering loudly on the machine in front of him. Her warning fallen on deaf ears and Florence couldn't help but worry as she hurried back to the house.

Later that night, just as she had suspected might happen, Miles started to look unwell over dinner.

"Have you put more coal than necessary on the fire, Sally? It seems unusually warm in the dining room this evening."

Sally looked startled and shook her head. "No, Master Miles, just what Mrs Moore told me to do. Penelope was busy helping Cook pluck the pheasants from the gamekeeper...but I'm sure I've done it right, Sir."

Florence gave her a sympathetic look. Since she had returned from Bath, Sally had realised that being spiteful to her was pointless and the two of them had reached an uneasy truce that had eventually turned into a friendship.

"I reckon you've overdone it today, Master Miles." Florence poured him a fresh glass of water.

"Sally's done nothing wrong. Maybe you're running a bit of a temperature?"

Miles tugged at his neckerchief, loosening it and Mrs DeVere gave him a worried look. "I'm still in two minds about this project of yours, Miles. I know I agreed not to interfere, and frankly, it's probably best I don't know what you're doing down there every day. I'm not good at keeping secrets from your Papa, but if it's going to make you ill, I will have to insist that you stop whatever this...this...thing is." She gestured vaguely in the direction of the western side of the estate, looking bemused.

"I'm fine, Mama...maybe it's just a bit of a chill. I'm sure a good night's sleep is all I need."

"Well, if you're quite sure." Evelyn took a spoonful of her parsnip soup, agreeing with him against her better judgement. "Just promise me you'll tell your Papa about it when he returns from London. You know he still wants you to oversee things more at Thruppley Mill, especially now that he's spending so much time away. You can't just keep saying no to him, without any justification."

"I'm almost ready to tell you both," Miles replied hastily. "I just need a few more weeks to get the final things in place."

"But what about the mill? Isn't there some way you could do that too? Collier can't run the place by himself...and he is just an employee, after all. It has always been a family-run business and your father is adamant it needs to continue that way." Evelyn had been grateful that Miles's secret project seemed to have given him a renewed sense of purpose in life, but she knew Robert would return to the thorny question of Miles working at the mill when he came back home again.

"I...I'll explain everything soon, Mama," Miles said, trying to reassure her. The truth was that he had no intention of working at the mill, but he knew his father wouldn't take no for an answer unless he could prove that he had a better idea instead. Everything rested on him getting the first machines up and running over the next few weeks.

* * *

"You have to stop and eat something, Miles. Look, Cook has made your favourite pheasant terrine, and I baked fresh crusty bread to go with it."

Florence didn't know whether to be irritated or concerned. For the last week, Miles had worked at the old mill building like a man possessed. He rose before dawn and rarely returned until after dark, taking a late meal in the library alone so he could pore over his drawings and notes.

Miles waved her away absentmindedly. "Just leave it there. I'll have something in a minute." His breath sounded wheezy and he put his hands on his knees, doubling over to cough. "It's just a bit of dust...nothing to worry about."

Jasper whined and nudged his nose against Miles's hand. His tail drooped and he turned to look at Florence with mournful brown eyes. It was seeing this that stiffened Florence's resolve.

"Miles. This can't go on," she cried. With a sigh, she put the basket of food down and guided Miles to the nearby chair, taking his sticks and propping them up against the machine. She put the back of her hand against his forehead. "If you're not careful you're going to get a fever. Didn't you learn anything from the last time this happened? You can be too stubborn for your own good."

Miles's shoulders slumped and he shook his head, defeated. "I'm so close to getting it done, Florence. If I can't show Papa a working machine after all these months, he'll dismiss my idea without even listening, I'm sure of it. Mama was right, he's going to expect an answer about me working at Thruppley Mill when he comes home."

Florence looked around at the cavernous old mill room. She and Penelope had whitewashed the walls, and the floorboards were spotless. The glass in the windows glinted in the low sun where she had polished them with vinegar and the long wooden worktable had been sanded and oiled ready for packing the chocolate.

"It's just the machinery that's holding you back, is it?" The spark of an idea was forming in her mind but she wasn't sure whether to mention it.

"Yes. You can see that everything else looks presentable, it's just this wretched machinery that's keeping me awake at night." He thumped the metal panel with frustration. "I can't afford to get a team of men in to help me, that's the problem."

"What about one person? I mean it's probably a silly idea, but—"

"Who do you have in mind?" Miles suddenly looked more hopeful. "Do you know someone who's handy at mending things?"

Florence grinned. "It just so happens, I do. But...he's...I don't want to speak out of turn...but he's had a challenging past. I mean he's a nice person," she added hastily. "But he probably won't have a reference from a previous employer, if that makes sense."

Miles looked puzzled and then nodded slowly, understanding her meaning. He scrambled to his feet with renewed zeal. "I won't ask any questions that might be awkward. As long as the fellow can mend this beast, that's good enough for me. When can he start?"

"I'll have to find him first," Florence chuckled. "Can I be excused to go into Chalsworth? I'll try and get an answer for you by the end of the day."

"Yes please, Florence. This could save everything." Miles ruffled Jasper's ears and the dog jumped up, licking his face excitedly. "Tell Mrs Moore that I've requested you collect something from Chalsworth for me, and ask Sawley to let you go on Bluebell. It will be quicker than walking and she's such an old plodder, you'll be fine."

"Are you sure? I'm only ridden a few times before." Florence looked alarmed and excited in equal measures.

"There's no time to spare. Bluebell is fine, if a little creaky these days. Just point her towards Chalsworth and enjoy the view," Miles added with a chuckle. "I learned to ride on her when I was tiny, don't worry, she'll look after you."

As Miles had said, Bluebell made Florence feel perfectly safe. Mr Sawley had held her reins while Florence scrambled inelegantly onto her broad back, hooking her leg over the high pommel of the ancient side saddle that still just about fitted the old mare. "It's like sitting on top of a table," Tom Sawley had joked. "Don't worry, she won't go faster than a trot. The only thing you have to be careful of is to make sure she doesn't steal an apple off the barrows when you go past the market. She's partial to a bit of cabbage too. Tie 'er up outside the church and give the lad there a penny and he'll look after 'er while you do what you need."

As the horse clopped over the cobbles coming into Chalsworth, Florence felt a sense of anticipation bubbling up inside her. She often bumped into Hunter when she came into town running errands for Mrs Moore. It had become such a habit to see him pop up when she least expected it that she had even wondered whether he looked out for her deliberately, before dismissing it as a fanciful notion. The way his hazel eyes held her gaze for a moment longer than was strictly necessary always made her feel unusually flustered, but he had never said anything to make her think his attention was more than just friendly interest.

"Do you know where I might find Hunter Rudge?" Florence handed a penny to the skinny urchin who was loitering outside the church as Tom had told her to.

"Hunter Rudge you say?" The boy scratched his head in a display of puzzlement. "I think so...although I dunno if I can be sure...it's hard to remember much when my stomach is rumblin' with hunger...all I can think about is those tasty pies on yonder stall, if only I had a penny to buy one." He scuffed the gaping toe of his boot against the cobbles and sighed extravagantly, waiting to see if she would get the message.

Florence couldn't help but smile at his wily ways. "There's another penny in it for you, if you can save me the time of looking all through town for him. And you'd be wise to remember I work for the DeVere family, so make sure you look after Bluebell properly, alright?"

The boy winked and tapped the side of his nose. "Of course. I know exactly who you are, Miss Florence, not much gets past me." He pointed towards a narrow street on the far corner of the market square. "Go to the end of Etnam Lane, and you'll see a small house with a green door. Reckon you might find Hunter there at this time of day."

He thrust his hand out for the extra money with a cheeky grin.

"You'll have it when I get back," Florence said firmly. "Take care of Bluebell, I won't be long."

"Right you are, Miss. One other thing...Josiah Rudge went to The Old Oak for some ale a little while ago...he likes to go most days. You probably want to make sure you're not still at his house if he decides to head home with a skinful of ale, if you get my meaning."

Florence felt a moment of trepidation as she approached the house the boy had directed her to. The further she got along Etnam Lane, the more ramshackle the houses became and she hoped that Hunter wouldn't mind her calling unannounced.

"Give us some coins, love...there's a good girl. I need a nip of gin to keep the cold out of my bones." A dirty hand clawed at Florence's dress from the shadow of one of the doorways and she stumbled back, shaking her head. "A curse on you then...you selfish wench." The woman spat at her and Florence hurried on.

That could have been me if it weren't for having a good job. The stark thought pricked Florence's conscience and she pulled a penny from her pocket, turning back to hand it to the woman.

"Thank you love...may you be blessed with a good 'usband and lots of nippers." The crone scuttled away in case Florence changed her mind.

"If only...but I'm not sure how I'll ever have that sort of happy ending," Florence muttered to herself with a wry smile. She rapped sharply on the green door, noticing that although the wood was rotting slightly at the bottom, the windows were sparkling clean and the doorstep had been freshly scrubbed.

"Who is it?" The door opened a crack and a freckled face gazed up at her.

"Hello. I'm Florence May. Is Hunter here? I need to speak to him."

The door opened slightly wider. "He's out the back. You're sure you ain't here about the rent?" The girl had the same flame-red hair as Josiah Rudge and looked to be about eight years old. She turned around as she heard scampering footsteps behind her and suddenly another smaller girl with the same red hair appeared in the doorway.

"You must be Hunter's younger sisters?" Florence smiled at them both.

"Are you his lady friend?" The younger of the two girls giggled then stuck her thumb in her mouth when the older one jabbed her sharply with her elbow.

"Hush, Mavis. You know Hunter told us not to talk to strangers." The older girl stared up at Florence again, as though assessing whether she could trust her. "Hunter ain't done nothing wrong, if anyone's asking."

"Are you going to invite her in, or not?" Hunter's deep voice sounded amused as he appeared behind them. "Florence, this is a nice surprise. I see you've already met the terrible two. This is Elsie, and the little one is Mavis...and they're supposed to be helping my Ma get dinner ready." He stood back and beckoned her off the street.

"Thank you...I'm sorry to call unexpectedly. I...I asked the boy outside the church who looks after the horses where I might find you...I hope you don't mind?" Florence took a deep breath, hoping Hunter wouldn't notice how flustered she felt.

"Will you have a cup of tea? Elsie, put the kettle on will you, and close your mouth or you might swallow a fly." He nudged Elsie ahead of them towards the kitchen. "We don't get many visitors, that's why they're being so nosy," he added with a grin.

Celia Rudge wiped her hands on her apron and darted a suspicious look between Florence and

Hunter. "What's she come for? You know your Pa might be back any minute and there'll be hell to pay if he sees her here."

"I'm sorry...I'll be quick." Florence wondered whether she'd made a terrible mistake. She didn't want to do anything to get Mrs Rudge or Hunter into trouble with Josiah and his bullying ways.

"It's alright Ma, I saw him going into the pub. He won't be back for hours."

Celia's frosty expression thawed slightly. "In that case, why don't you sit down and Elsie will pour the tea." She reached to the top shelf of the dresser pulling down the only cup that didn't have a chip on the rim and polished it on her apron.

Florence gave her a warm smile. "That's very kind of you." Clearly, Celia was a houseproud woman, even though the furniture all looked as though it had seen better days. There were three armchairs in front of the small hearth, and several stitched samplers hanging on the wall.

"We ain't got much, but we make do with what we have," Celia commented, following Florence's gaze. "I used to enjoy a bit of sewing when I was younger. Don't have time for it now though, I'm too busy charring. Hunter takes good care of us though." She lifted her chin, looking proudly at her son.

Elsie and Mavis sat at the scrubbed table, watching Florence curiously, with wide eyes. "She looks very pretty, don't she." Mavis whispered loudly behind her hand, making Elsie giggle.

Florence sipped her tea, not knowing what to say.

"Now then, you two...you know it's not polite to talk about people, even if what you said is perfectly true." Hunter put a hand on each of his sisters' shoulders and looked at them fondly and Florence felt herself blushing at the compliment.

"Are you still mending things for a living?" she asked.

Celia's expressions instantly became guarded at her question. "Why do you want to know. Hunter works harder than anyone to keep this roof over our heads and food on our table, but what he does to earn his money is nobody's business but ours." She crossed her arms and looked pointedly at the clock on the mantelshelf. "We don't have time to sit around chatting like the folk at Bisley Court, you know."

"Ma, give the poor girl a chance to speak. She's a hard-working person, like us, you know."

Florence shot Hunter a grateful glance. "I'll get to the point of my visit," she said hastily. "Master DeVere needs help to mend some machinery and I told him that you're very good at that sort of thing. He could pay you for a few weeks' work if you'd be interested—"

"It's out of the question. Hunter can't work at Bisley Court, he's far too busy." Celia Rudge's reply was curt, stopping Florence mid-sentence.

"Actually, I haven't got too much on at the moment, Ma. The extra money for Christmas would be helpful, don't you think? If it means you don't have to take on extra charring work, I think it's a good idea." Hunter sipped his tea thoughtfully, standing with his back to the meagre fire. He glanced at the half-empty coal bucket to underline his point.

Celia's hands fidgeted in her lap as she twisted the corner of her apron. Her expression showed how conflicted she felt. "I was hoping your Pa might turn over a new leaf and look for a new job...he got the sack over a silly disagreement with the factory foreman, you see," she explained to Florence.

"You mean he started a fight again...and spends every penny he can get his hands on in the pub,"

Hunter said bitterly. "You deserve better than him, Ma," he added. His tone was weary as though this was a conversation they had had many times.

Florence followed Hunter's worried gaze as he glanced at his mother's cheek. She realised that there was an angry purple bruise just under her hairline that looked as though it had only happened in the last day or so. Celia tugged on her hair self-consciously, trying to hide it and Florence's heart went out to her.

"Master DeVere won't ask any awkward questions, and the work itself isn't in Bisley Court as such. It's in an old mill building that's hidden away in the woods. He told me to tell you that the pay will be good."

"And you're sure Hunter won't see any of the DeVere family apart from the son?" Celia asked fretfully.

"I very much doubt it, Mrs Rudge. It's a project Master DeVere is working on alone, but his health is poor and he desperately needs some help to finish before Christmas."

Hunter sat down at the table and put his hand over his mother's to reassure her. "I should probably explain our reticence," he said, turning to look at Florence once his mother had given him a small nod. "Pa used to work at Thruppley Mill many years ago, but they sent him packing. He never told Ma why...just said that they had wronged him. He swore that he would never have anything to do with the DeVere family ever again...or any of us would, for that matter."

"He was ever so angry that time he saw Hunter talking to you in the street," Celia muttered. "Just knowing that you worked for the DeVere family was all it took to set his temper off." Her expression was pinched and she suddenly clasped Hunter's hand. "I know we need the money, but no good will come of it, Hunter. You must stay away from them."

Hunter stood up and paced around the room. "Ma, I'm tired of picking pockets to make up for Pa's laziness and bad temper."

"Shussh, Hunter...don't say that." Celia clutched her hand to her throat looking scared.

"It's alright Ma, Florence has always known what I do...who I am. But I don't want to be like that anymore, can't you understand?" He sat back down at the table and looked between his mother and Florence with a determined expression. "Pa need never know about this work, and if Florence says Master DeVere is trustworthy then I'll take her word for it. I want to make a better life for you and the girls, Ma, and I'll never be able to do that if I carry on thieving to get by. This could be the new start that I need. I'm going to do it," he added firmly.

Florence grinned at him, happy that she had been able to give him this opportunity. "That's wonderful. And I promise Master DeVere is a very kind person, Mrs Rudge. He'll be so grateful for Hunter's help. Can I tell him you'll start tomorrow?"

Celia Rudge nodded reluctantly, knowing when she was beaten. "I hope we don't live to regret this," she muttered, gulping down the last of her tea. "As long as it's just this once and you promise to steer clear of everyone else at Bisley Court."

"It will be fine, Ma. Maybe we can even have a few treats for Christmas this year with the extra money." Hunter gave her a hug, but Florence could tell that Celia was still stricken with worry.

CHAPTER 14

"Hold that part steady, while I hammer in these nails." The air filled with the deafening sound of metal on metal and Florence clapped her hands over her ears until it had finished.

"Look how much progress we've made." Miles stuck his head up from where he had clambered into the bowels of the machine and waved at Florence as she draped a cloth over the nearby table to unpack their lunch.

"Well, don't expect me to know what any of this stuff does, but if you say you're making progress then that makes me very happy." She poured out the thick dark coffee she had made into three mugs and threw a couple of logs into the stove, sending a shower of sparks up the chimney.

"We'd have got more done if Master DeVere didn't talk so much." Hunter grinned at Miles to show that his words were good-natured.

"I've told you not to call me that...you've helped me so much I consider you to be a friend now, just like Florence. While we're down here, I'm just Miles, not Master DeVere, alright?"

Miles swung his legs slowly out of the machine and carefully reversed down the wooden ladder propped up against it and Florence passed him his walking sticks. She noticed that he seemed less shaky than he had been during the summer. All the physical work had made his muscles stronger and she wondered if they could dare to hope that he might not need his sticks for much longer.

The three of them sat at the table and Florence passed round the hunks of buttered bread with a wedge of crumbly cheese and a slice of ham, along with a dollop of Cook's finest damson pickle.

"It's Hunter's fault that I talk too much," Miles explained to Florence with a burst of laughter. "He's given me so many good ideas for the chocolate factory, my head is overflowing with even more plans. Every time I get stuck, Hunter helps me think of a better solution."

"I enjoy thinking about this sort of thing," Hunter mumbled through his mouthful of food, gesturing at the machines.

"Well, if all you normally do is mend machinery, your talents are wasted," Miles replied. "You're just a smart as any of the foremen at Thruppley Mill from what I know of them, I can tell you. I even want to tell Papa about some of the good ideas you've come up with to help us operate more efficiently."

"Oh I don't think you'll want to bother him with that," Hunter said hastily, his eyes clouding with alarm.

"Hunter prefers to be behind the scenes, Miles...remember what I told you..." Florence darted a warning look at him and Miles immediately looked contrite.

"I know I said I wouldn't ask about your past, Hunter, and I'm a man of my word. It's just that I think you're capable of more than you give yourself credit for. You could look for a better job...I'd put in a good reference for you."

Hunter shrugged. "That's kind of you to say so, but my options are limited. I can't move away and leave my family. They rely on me, and that's all there is to it. It was good of you to offer me this work though, don't think I'm being ungrateful."

He smiled at Florence and she felt her heart skip a beat. She had grown to look forward to their lunches together and she realised with a sinking feeling that she would miss him when the job was finished.

"Maybe Miles might have more work for you, at some point?"

"I'll certainly keep you in mind," Miles said, nodding. "It has been nice having your company these last few weeks...I know we're from different walks of life but you seem to see things in a similar way to me. Once the chocolate factory has become established and profitable, maybe you could work here?"

"I'll have to see if Ma thinks it's alright," Hunter said, not committing himself.

As soon as they had finished lunch, Florence packed up the basket and rolled up her sleeves to get to work scrubbing the floor in the small room off to the side where the cocoa beans would be roasted. Miles had spoken to Mrs Moore, telling her that Florence was needed on his project several days each week and much to Florence's surprise, Mrs Moore had pursed her lips and reluctantly agreed. "She always did have a soft spot for Master Miles," Cook had remarked as she trickled more brandy on the Christmas cake.

The good-natured chatter from Hunter and Miles in the room next door made Florence glad that he had agreed to do the work. The two of them got on so well, in spite of Hunter's initial reservations that Miles would be just like every other well-to-do gentleman who expected the poorer classes to do their bidding.

As she lathered up the soap in the bucket of water and scrubbed the flagstones with the stiff bristled brush, the rhythmic motion allowed Florence's thoughts to drift.

I wonder what it would be like to be married to Hunter, living in a little cottage in the countryside... Her mouth curved into a smile as her imagination ran away with her. She pictured Hunter walking up the path at the end of his working day, swinging her off her feet and bending his head to kiss—

Suddenly her delightful daydream was interrupted by the urgent thrum of galloping hooves approaching. She jumped up to peer through the window wondering who was coming in such haste and the blood froze in her veins.

Mr DeVere was outside the old mill building with a face like thunder as his horse pranced under him, full of nervous energy. He jumped nimbly from its back and tied the reins on the nearest tree. "Stand still," he commanded, and then he turned to look at the building and swiped his whip through the air in a gesture of annoyance.

"Miles...your Papa is outside." Florence shouted a warning but their hammering was too loud for them to hear. She darted across the soapy floor, almost losing her balance, then burst into the room where Miles and Hunter were working. "Mr DeVere has come back from London early...he's here!" Florence cried, trying to get Miles's attention.

Hunter jumped down off the ladder to leave but it was too late. Robert DeVere threw the door open and stood on the threshold, surveying the scene in front of him with a look of incredulity.

"What the devil do you think you're doing?" He strode into the room and Florence's heart sank. His eyes narrowed with anger and he slapped his whip on the machine, sending Miles's sticks clattering across the floor.

"Papa? I thought you weren't returning for a few more weeks?"

"So it would appear," Mr DeVere snapped. "I thought it would be a nice surprise for your mother, given that I've been away for so long. I expected you to be in the library but Mr Middleton told me you're here most days. Would you care to tell me exactly what's been going on in my absence? I don't recall giving you my approval for any of this."

"I...I wanted to show you...I've almost finished...it's an idea I've had for a while that I believe would be..."

"Would you stop stuttering and get to the point, Miles. I turn my back for a few months and rather than showing an interest in Thruppley Mill as I'd hoped, you...you put all your time into this...this...harebrained idea." He looked around the room with a scornful expression.

Miles flushed and he lifted his chin, determined not to be browbeaten. "I've done all the figures, Papa. It's not a stupid idea, it's going to be a proper business. This old building was sitting here doing nothing, so I knew you wouldn't miss it. I've worked day and night to restore it, and it's going to be a chocolate factory."

"Chocolate? What the...why?" Mr DeVere's mouth gaped open and he let out a snort of contempt. "What a ridiculous idea. I always suspected you were a namby-pamby fool but this is absurd—"

"I think that's a bit harsh, Sir. Master DeVere's idea is excellent if you don't mind me saying." Hunter stepped forward, unable to stop himself from commenting.

"I beg your pardon? How dare you question what I say." Mr DeVere glared at Hunter. "Who is this insolent fellow?" he demanded, turning back to Miles.

"Oh, he's someone I asked to help me, so I could finish getting everything ready in time for your return."

"My name is Hunter Rudge, Sir. I meant no disrespect. I've been working with Master DeVere to repair the machinery and although I'm no expert, his business plan sounds very well thought out." Hunter stuck his hand out to shake hands but Mr DeVere's eyes had darkened even more.

"Rudge? Did you say Hunter Rudge? If that's the case, you can leave this instant, without any pay."

"Papa! That's not fair. I asked Hunter to help

me and he's been nothing but professional." Miles looked shocked and Florence thought for one moment that Mr DeVere might strike him with the whip too, for defying him.

"Be quiet, boy. You don't know what you're talking about. Josiah Rudge stole from me at Thruppley Mill, many years ago. He was a lying, conniving scoundrel and I vowed never to have dealings with any member of the Rudge family ever again."

Hunter quickly gathered up his tools and stuffed them into his bag, swinging it over his shoulder. "As you wish, Mr DeVere. I'll not stay where I'm not wanted." He turned and shook Miles's hand and darted an apologetic look towards Florence.

"Get along with you," Mr DeVere snapped again. "I can see I need to take a firm hand on things again here at Bisley Court. Standards have been slipping and I won't tolerate it."

"Just one last thing," Hunter said, turning back to them on his way out. "You'd do well to remember that I did this to help your son...who is a gentleman through and through. I might be a Rudge, but that doesn't mean I'm tarred with the same brush as something that happened all those years ago, does it?" He took the steps two at a time and strode across the field without so much as a backward glance.

Miles sat down heavily in the chair and sighed. "Do we have to fight Papa? Won't you at least let me tell you about my idea? I promise I've looked into it from every angle...I genuinely think it will be a profitable business, and quite quickly too."

Mr DeVere walked slowly around the machine, pausing now and again to look at parts of it more closely. "Did you do most of this yourself? The last time I came here was years ago and the place looked almost derelict. I remember the stories my father told me about how the business started from this little building." He sounded almost reflective now that Hunter had gone.

"Yes, I did a lot of it, Papa. With some help from Florence...in fact I couldn't have done it without her."

Mr DeVere glanced in Florence's direction as though only just noticing her. "I'm pleased to see you've mended your ways," he commented, with a slight smile. "My wife told me you were a hard worker, even if you do speak your mind when you shouldn't."

Miles stood up again and Florence hurried to pass him his sticks.

"Once we've had dinner, I suppose it wouldn't harm to look through your ideas," Mr DeVere said grudgingly. "I must warn you though...I shall be looking at them with a critical eye...no favours just because you're my son. If the business doesn't make financial sense, I won't support you, is that clear? Especially as we already have a perfectly good business in the form of Thruppley Mill that I had hoped you would take on, in time."

Miles nodded and picked up his hammer again. "Thank you, Papa. I won't disappoint you."

* * *

THE FOLLOWING MORNING, Miles was bubbling with excitement as he limped towards the kitchen to fetch Florence. The evening had gone better than he had hoped and his father had finally conceded that perhaps his idea was not such a bad one after all.

"Are you ready to go, Florence? Now that Papa knows everything we don't need to keep it a secret any longer."

Cook drained a pan of boiled swede in the sink

and steam billowed around her head. "Thank goodness for that, Master Miles. It's not right keeping secrets in the family like that; they have a way of coming home to roost."

"I'm sorry Mrs Williams." Miles looked apologetic. "I just wanted to surprise Papa...besides it was all those afternoons in the kitchen when you used to let me help you that first gave me the idea."

Cook looked at him fondly. "You mean when we used to make chocolate fancies? They were always your favourites."

"Exactly," Miles replied with a chuckle. "And thank you for being so patient letting me borrow Florence to help me. It won't be for much longer, I promise."

The grass crunched under their feet as Florence and Miles walked down to the old mill together. There had been a hard frost overnight and the landscape looked as though it had been dipped in diamonds, glittering in the hazy winter sunshine.

"I'm sorry Papa reacted the way he did with Hunter." Miles paused for a moment to catch his breath before they continued into the woods. "He can be a very stubborn man at times, as you've probably realised. If he thinks someone has wronged him...well...he doesn't believe in second chances."

"Hunter is nothing like his father," Florence said firmly. "I can understand that Mr DeVere took offence at Mr Rudge's behaviour, but it did seem very unfair to tar Hunter with the same brush."

"I tried to put in a good word for him, Florence, I promise. But Papa's mind was made up. I told him that Hunter had a rare talent, for more than just machines too. Maybe he'll listen to me more once he's got accustomed to the idea of the chocolate factory."

"He works very hard to look after his Ma and his younger sisters." Florence tightened her shawl as a chilly wind picked up.

"I can see he's very fond of you," Miles replied, raising one eyebrow. "I hope he doesn't dally with your affections though. I'd hate to see you get hurt if he goes back to his...less honest ways of making a living."

"We're just friends, Miles, that's all."

Florence walked faster to hide the blush which had crept over her cheeks. She wasn't ready to share the tiny seed of a dream that one day she and Hunter could become more than friends. Even when she had last seen Dulcie, whose head was filled with thoughts of romance since Norman Crocker had declared he would like to make Dulcie his wife, Florence had kept her yearnings for love a secret.

As they rounded the corner, Florence was surprised to see that the door to the old mill was already open. "Did somebody already start work?" She waited for Miles to catch up.

"I'm sure I didn't leave the place open last night, although I must confess I was so shocked by Papa's visit that I might have forgotten to lock up. Not to worry, nobody ever comes down here except us."

As they let themselves in, Miles let out a groan of dismay. "Oh no! All my hard work is ruined." He stumbled forward on his sticks and Florence grabbed his arm to steady him. She flung open the shutters on the windows and as the light streamed in, the full extent of what had happened made her gasp with shock. The machine which had been so nearly finished now lay in pieces, scattered across the floor, and trampled into the floorboards.

"How could this have happened?" Florence cried.

Miles shook his head sorrowfully. "They've even stolen some of the pieces of the pistons...it's just so spiteful." He walked slowly around the debris and his shoulders drooped with frustration.

"Can they be replaced? Will you be able to fix it again?" Florence's mind filled with questions, but the one she didn't dare to utter, pulsed through her head. *Who did this?*

Miles knelt awkwardly on the floor and started gathering the nuts and bolts, shoving them into his pockets, without speaking. The silence stretched between them until Florence couldn't bear it a moment longer.

"Say it then...I know what you're thinking."

Miles scrambled to his feet. "There's only one person who this could have been, and I'm as disappointed as you are, Florence. It must have been Hunter, because Papa refused to pay him. Who else could it have been?"

Florence opened her mouth to protest Hunter's innocence, then closed it again with a sigh. Every part of her being wanted to believe that he was a reformed man, but the evidence said otherwise. She felt tears prickling behind her eyes and blinked them away.

What's the point in crying for something that could never be, she thought with a heavy heart. Clearly,

Hunter had turned out to be no better than his father, after all.

She hurried around the room, picking up the pieces as quickly as she could, trying to right the wrongs that had been done to Miles. "You can fix it again," she said stoutly. "It's just a setback, that's all. Maybe Mr Sawley can help you instead...he's good at mending things...and young Tom can help too. We'll get it all sorted, Miles. Now is not the time to give up."

Miles smiled at her. "There you go again, looking on the bright side." He nodded slowly and rolled his sleeves up. "You're right. It won't take long to get back to where we were. Even if I have to ask Papa for some money to replace what's been stolen."

Florence swallowed the lump in her throat and hummed as she worked. She didn't want Miles to know how hurt she felt that Hunter had betrayed her trust, throwing everything back in her face as though it was of no consequence.

Could it really be him that did this? Didn't our friendship mean anything? The thoughts swirled through her mind, leaving her with more questions than answers. She had been so sure that Hunter was a kind, decent person, it shocked her that she had been so wrong. Her thought drifted to Dulcie and Norman's summer wedding that they had planned, and Miles and Cora being so much in love and she blinked back the tears that threatened again. These last few weeks, she had fallen in love with Hunter...there was no denying it. But she had to face up to the fact that she would have to put him out of her mind...even though every part of her still longed to see that warm smile of his and the way his hazel eyes lingered when he looked at her as if she meant everything to him.

CHAPTER 15

"*A*re you going to help decorate the tree after dinner tonight?" Cook pushed a cup of tea across the table and gave Florence an encouraging smile.

"Say yes, Florence, it will be fun."

"Go on, you've been so quiet these last few weeks, I don't know what's got into you."

Dulcie and Sally looked at her expectantly and giggled. Mr Sawley had dragged a huge tree into the main hallway of Bisley Court the day before, carefully standing it in its usual place in the corner.

"Mrs DeVere said you three could decorate it...you know she often feels low at this time of year. It's quite an honour that she's letting you do

245

it, you know." Cook gave Florence a worried glance. She knew something was bothering her, but when she had gently asked her what was wrong, Florence had muttered that it was nothing. She wondered whether it was to do with that business that had happened down at the old mill a few weeks ago.

"Will you let us have a glass of eggnog after we've done it?" Sally grinned and nudged Dulcie. "Maybe your Norman might have some mistletoe to kiss you under, now that you're engaged to be married."

"Don't go putting ideas into her head," Cook said hastily. "Dulcie's far too sensible to get carried away like that...anyway we don't want any babies until well after the wedding, do we dear," she added firmly, making Dulcie blush.

Florence gathered their breakfast dishes and took them to the sink to start washing up. She found that keeping busy was the only way to stop herself from thinking about Hunter, and now that it was only a few days before Christmas, there was plenty to do around the house to distract herself.

"I can't believe we'll be getting everything ready for Miles and Cora's wedding in a few months. It's such a long time since we last had a big celebration here." Cook sipped her tea as she reminisced. "I miss the old days, before...the fire. The DeVere family used to be so sociable. We would have hunting parties in the winter, a summer ball, we'd be preparing for weeks and the house would look so beautiful with vases of flowers and bunting.

"Maybe once Master DeVere is married and they have children, Mrs DeVere might not feel so sad every Christmas," Sally ventured. "I can't imagine how terrible it must have been for the family, losing one of their children that way."

"Well, let's do what we can to bring a bit of festive cheer to the house and hope that Mrs DeVere feels happier soon." Cook stood up quickly and told Dulcie and Sally to go and fetch the decorations from the cupboard in the attic where they were stored, to try and dispel the air of gloom which had crept over them.

"Florence, you and Penelope can help me make the eggnog after you've done the washing up. And ask Mr Middleton to get some port out of the cellar. Master Miles has been working so hard, it's about time he rested for a few days and enjoyed himself."

Florence and Penelope made short work of the washing up and Florence bustled through to the library to see if Miles would be eating dinner with the family that night.

Miles smiled as she pushed the door open. "Just the person I want to see." He pointed at the ledger in front of him. "Look, Papa and I have done the figures and he's agreed that I can begin buying in the cocoa beans to start making chocolate in a few weeks. It's really happening Florence!"

"So soon? I know you'd made good progress catching up after...after what happened to the machines, but I didn't realise you were so close to starting." She threw a log on the fire and the sparks flew up the chimney filling the room with the comforting scent of applewood smoke.

"I can hardly believe it myself either." Miles sighed happily and leant back in his chair, stretching his arms. "Papa is still upset that I'm not going to work at Thruppley Mill, but I've persuaded him to give me a chance for one year. If I can make the chocolate factory profitable in that time, he said he'll just ask Mr Collier to take on more work instead."

"And what about Cora? She must be so proud of everything you've achieved. You'll have to give her the grand tour when they arrive."

Miles suddenly jumped up from his chair and

smacked his hand on his forehead. "Cora! I've been so busy with the factory, I completely forgot to collect her Christmas present from Chalsworth. I've commissioned the silversmith to make a brooch for her." He turned to look at Florence with a pleading expression, making her laugh.

"You're incorrigible, Miles. You can't be that forgetful once you're married you know, Cora won't let you get away with it." She put her hands on her hips. "Go on then, I suppose you want me to get it for you? As if I haven't got enough on my plate already."

"I'd be ever so grateful, Florence. I would have sent Tom Sawley, but the brooch is rather valuable and I'm not sure he'd be up to the task. I know I can trust you implicitly and you could even choose a nice piece of ribbon to tie around the present up as well. I could hardly expect Tom to do that, could I?" Miles smiled even wider, knowing that Florence would agree.

"Oh alright then," she chuckled. "If you ask Mr Sawley to get Bluebell ready, I'll go just as soon as I've laid the fire in your bedroom and checked that Penelope is getting the guest bedrooms ready.

As Bluebell plodded towards Chalsworth an hour later, Florence thought about everything that had happened over the last few weeks. She hadn't seen Hunter on her last few visits to town and it had left an empty ache in her heart.

At least he could have explained why he did it...maybe I could have understood...even forgiven him if he apologised. The thought slid into her mind and the more she considered it, the more she felt a sense of frustration growing inside her. Hunter didn't seem the type to shy away from difficult conversations but he had vanished from her life like a fox slinking away in the morning light.

Chalsworth was busy and there was a festive air in the market square. The costermongers shouted more loudly than usual, and the aroma of roasting chestnuts from the brazier near the church made Florence's mouth water. She squeezed past the other shoppers, laughing as a gaggle of rosy-cheeked children clapped excitedly at the punch and judy show the owner of the toyshop was performing to attract a crowd.

"Try our Christmas pudding...it's got more currants in it than ever before."

"Get 'yer fresh goose today and I'll throw in a tasty rasher of bacon for the pot."

"Sprig of heather to bring you good luck, m'lady?"

Florence nodded to all the folk who were hawking their wares, hurrying onwards until she reached the calmness of the silversmith's shop. The bell tinkled as she entered and an elderly man looked up at her from behind the counter. His eyes looked enormous through the magnifying glass he was using, making her smile. "I'm here to collect the brooch you've made for Master DeVere." Florence handed over the letter Miles had given her, in case the silversmith was reluctant to give it to her, plus the pouch of coins which was the balance of what he owed.

"I've just finished it...and very pretty it is too." The old man rubbed his hands and pulled a small velvet box from the drawer. "Mind you keep it safe on the way home," he added. He popped the lid open and admired his handiwork one last time before handing it over to Florence.

"Thank you, Sir. And you can rest assured I'll take good care of it. I'm going straight back to Bisley Court now." Florence tucked the box into a hidden internal pocket in her dress and stepped back out onto the street. She paused for a moment to look across the market square hoping that she might spot Hunter, but he wasn't there and she felt a sting of disappointment.

"Ready to leave again so soon, Miss Florence?" The boy minding Bluebell looked surprised to see her again so quickly. "I thought you'd be spending longer, what with it being nearly Christmas. I only just gave Bluebell a nosebag of oats to eat." He stamped his feet to get warm, glancing up at the leaden sky.

"I don't mind waiting," Florence replied. Bluebell deserved a treat. The church bell chimed the hour and the first snowflakes started to drift down, dusting her cloak. "Maybe I'll go into the church for a few minutes." She passed the boy his penny and walked briskly through the lych gate.

"Good day, my dear." The vicar, Mr Jerome, looked up from where he had been arranging the prayer books, pleased to see an unexpected visitor. "Are you here to pray or taking shelter from the snow?"

Florence coughed to cover her embarrassment that he had guessed her reason for coming into the church outside of the regular Sunday service. "I...I thought I might light a candle to remember my parents by if that's alright?"

"Of course it is Florence." He smiled at her. "You don't need an excuse to come into the church, you know. God's house is always open for those in need."

Florence walked to the back of the church and carefully lit a new candle with a taper. As the tiny flame wavered then shone more strongly, she tried to think of a prayer to say for her parents, but her mind stayed stubbornly blank. "I can't even remember what you look like, Ma," she whispered. She felt tears stinging her eyes and surreptitiously wiped them away.

"Is something troubling you, my child?" The vicar glided serenely to Florence's side and opened his hands, inviting her to reply.

Florence sighed. "I...I thought I'd found someone who was a true friend...which is a rare thing when you're an orphan like me."

The vicar nodded, not saying anything.

"But...something happened...I want to believe that he's a good person...but now I just don't know. Maybe I was a fool to trust him." She shrugged and tried to smile but Mr Jerome laid a gentle hand on her arm.

"You're a kindhearted girl, Florence. Maybe if you speak to him you'll get to the bottom of things. We all do things we regret...perhaps your friend just needs you to give him a second chance, eh?"

Florence sighed again and realised the vicar was right. She had to find out for herself why Hunter had stolen from Miles otherwise she would never be able to put her mind at rest, no matter what his reasons were.

"Take a moment and think of what you truly want, Florence. The Lord is listening to you if you have the courage to tell him what you wish for." The vicar smiled at her again and drifted away.

Florence gazed at the candle again, noticing how the flickering flame pierced the gloom and held her eyes as though she was hypnotised. "I wish...I wish that Miles could be well again...and that Mrs DeVere could find happiness. I wish...that I could always be part of Bisley Court...and that I can find it in my heart to forgive Hunter so we can perhaps be friends again one day." She closed her eyes and the image of the candle flame lingered in her mind. "Thank you, dear Lord, for hearing my prayer today."

When Florence came back outside, the snow was falling harder and starting to settle. She ran down the path, feeling happier than she had for weeks. The vicar's words had given her comfort and she knew exactly what she had to do. "Look after Bluebell for a bit longer please, Alf. There's

THE MAID'S WINTER WISH

somewhere I have to go." Florence passed the boy another penny and ran to Etman Lane as fast as she could on the slippery cobbles.

As she reached the green door of the Rudge's house, Florence skidded to a halt and tilted her head backwards, looking up into the sky. *Come on, what have you got to lose?* The words in her mind gave her courage as the snowflakes swirled down, making her feel dizzy. She pressed her hands together, offering up a hurried prayer again. *Please Lord...show me that Hunter is the good-hearted man I thought him to be.* The snow fell harder and she took a deep breath, rapping sharply at the door.

"Mavis, come quick, Florence has come to visit again." Elsie stood in the doorway with a wide smile. "Mavis likes you," she stated baldly. She scuffed her toe on the threadbare doormat before looking up shyly again. "I like you too. We were hoping you might call again, but Hunter said we weren't to keep asking him when you were coming back."

"Is Hunter home?" Florence asked hastily before she lost her nerve. There was something about Elsie's forthright manner that was refreshing and she realised with a wry smile that

Elsie reminded her of herself when she was that age.

"Come in and I'll fetch him for you. Ma's upstairs because she's...not feeling very well." Elsie took Florence's hand and pulled her into the house as though she was worried she might leave again. "I've made some soup for me and Mavis, all by myself. I have to take care of her when Ma's taken to her bed, but I don't mind."

Florence noticed that the room wasn't as tidy as the last time she had visited. The coal bucket was almost empty and the doors of the small dresser hung off their hinges.

"Pa gave us all a row last night," Elsie said, following Florence's gaze. "Me and Mavis hide upstairs when he's like that if we can get away quick enough." She rubbed her arm and her expression clouded.

Florence felt a ripple of alarm. Clearly, Josiah Rudge wasn't only a violent bully towards his wife. The way Elsie was holding herself told her that there were probably bruises under her thin dress and her heart went out to the two little girls.

"Who is it?"

The sound of Hunter's voice made Florence's breath catch in her throat. Suddenly she wondered if she had done the wrong thing, coming to confront him in his own home.

"This is a lovely surprise. Don't mind me, I was covered in soot and Elsie told me I had to have a wash or she wouldn't give me any lunch." Hunter sauntered into the room, drying his chest on a rag.

Florence blushed as she caught sight of his broad shoulders and well-defined muscles. She noticed that he had a large scar on the side of his ribs where the skin was puckered and silvery and she averted her eyes quickly, not wanting him to think she was staring.

"How is everything progressing with the chocolate factory?" Hunter asked as he slipped his shirt back on. "I'm sorry I left so quickly the other day. Mr DeVere was in no mood to listen to anything I had to say, so it seemed like the sensible thing to do. I hoped I might bump into you in Chalsworth, but...things have been difficult at home and I've been busy trying to take on a few extra odd jobs to make up for the money that DeVere didn't pay me."

"Would you like a cuppa tea?" Elsie tugged on Florence's hand, hoping she would say yes.

Florence nodded, suddenly lost for words and she tried to gather her thoughts. Hunter must take her for a fool if he was brazenly pretending that that day had been the last time he'd been at Bisley Manor. She felt a surge of anger that he was being so nonchalant about it all.

"What about all the damage you did to the machine?" she demanded. "Miles was devastated that you ruined all his hard work...and stole from him as well, to make matters worse. I've come against my better judgement to hear it from you. Why did you do it, Hunter?"

Hunter's face creased with confusion. "Do what? I don't know what you're talking about."

"The day after Mr DeVere sent you away...you know...don't deny it. Somebody damaged the machine and stole pieces of the piston. It must have been you." Florence paced around the small room, feeling disappointment curdling in her stomach.

The kettle screeched as it came to a boil and Elsie poured the water with shaking hands. "Please don't argue," she pleaded, looking beseechingly at Florence. "Hunter ain't done nothing wrong."

Hunter stepped forwards and took Florence's hands in his, looking deep into her eyes. "I promise it wasn't me, Florence. You have to believe me." He shook his head and his expression hardened as he came to a sudden realisation. "The day after I left, you say you discovered it? Now it all makes sense."

"What...what do you mean Hunter. If you didn't do it, then who did? Nobody else knew about the work you were doing at the old mill."

"Pa knew," Hunter blurted out angrily. "He overheard me telling Ma what had happened and then he stormed out. We thought he's just gone to the pub like he always does. But he didn't come home that night, and he had a pocketful of coins when I saw him in town the next day. He was crowing on about getting his own back, but I didn't heed his words...I thought they were just drunken ramblings."

It took a moment for Hunter's words to sink in, but when they did, Florence felt as though a weight had been lifted from her shoulders. "It wasn't you then? I've been so upset, thinking you'd betrayed my trust and done something so hurtful...to me and to Miles as well."

"Never, Florence. I'd never do anything like that to Miles, or to hurt you...I love you." Hunter gave a shaky laugh and stroked Florence's cheek.

Florence stepped back in shock. "Are you really sure Hunter? You're not just saying it? I don't know what to believe anymore." She gazed into his hazel eyes and her mind buzzed with confusion. "You've always been a pickpocket Hunter, ever since I've known you...you make your living by being dishonest. I want to trust you...but I can't."

Hunter's eyes clouded with hurt and he nodded slowly. "I can't deny that, Florence. Everything you say about me being a pickpocket is true...but I don't steal from people anymore. I haven't for a long time, in fact. But you only have my word for it and if you believe I'm a bad person, I can't say anything to change your mind."

Florence looked at him, not knowing what to say. "I need to be able to trust you, Hunter. If there's to be any future for us...I love you too. I always have...but—"

"That's all I need to know for now," Hunter said, breaking into a smile. "We love each other..." He pulled her into his arms and held her tight.

Florence felt giddy with emotion as she felt their hearts beating together. She returned his embrace, but he suddenly winced as her sleeve scratched against his ribs where she had seen the scar. "I'm sorry...I didn't mean to hurt you."

"It's nothing," Hunter chuckled. "I've had it for as long as I can remember, it just aches a bit when the weather is cold."

Florence smiled up at him, wishing she could stay in his arms forever. "I want to believe what you've told me, Hunter, I really do. But Miles was so upset."

Hunter gently let her go. "I'll prove it to you, Florence. If it's the last thing I do. You mean everything to me and I understand why you're hesitant to trust me." He shrugged and his face was etched with regret and longing. "I want you to look at me with love and pride, if we're ever to be together... which is my dream...not mistrust, always wondering if I'm going to turn out like my wretched Pa."

Florence nodded her understanding, also full of regret. "We're not children anymore Hunter. We can't pretend that stealing buttons is all a bit of fun." Her eyes misted with unshed tears and she ran from the room, letting herself out of the house and stumbling through the streets back to Bluebell and her life in Bisley Court.

CHAPTER 16

"*P*ass me up the candles, Penelope."
Sally wobbled on the stepladder
next to the Christmas tree and Dulcie leapt
forward to steady it.

"I've almost finished threading the dried orange
slices," Tom muttered from where he was sitting
cross-legged next to the tray that Cook had
brought from the kitchen.

Florence carefully unwrapped the delicate glass
baubles from the soft wool they nestled in and
hung them on the prickly branches. As much as
she wanted to enjoy the moment, her mind was
full of the conversation she had had with Hunter
earlier that day.

"Here's the eggnog we promised you. Tom and

Penelope, you're not old enough, so you can have some of my spiced apple juice." The hallway filled with the scent of cinnamon and cloves as Cook placed the tray of drinks on the sideboard.

"Just a couple more, then we're finished." Sally stretched up and added the last few candles to the pine fronds, adjusting the sparkly tinsel as she stepped back down the ladder.

"Well, this looks very festive indeed." Mrs Moore hurried from the library, clutching the list of everything that needed to be done that never left her side. "Penelope, did you take the warming pans up for the beds in the guest bedrooms? The Ellwood family will be arriving on Boxing Day and I want to make sure the beds aren't damp. Those rooms can get very chilly at this time of year."

"Yes, Mrs Moore." Penelope nodded enthusiastically. Her face was pink with excitement as she looked at the tree.

"I do hope Mrs DeVere will feel better by tomorrow." Cook's brow furrowed with worry as she spoke quietly to Mrs Moore. "That business down at the old mill with the Rudge boy has brought everything flooding back. It took me right back to that terrible time as well. Poor Mrs

DeVere, she's struggling more than ever with missing Hugo this year."

Florence's ears pricked up as she heard them talking about Hunter and she edged closer under the guise of pouring the spiced apple drinks out for Penelope and Tom.

"I know, 'tis a terrible business. I always felt sorry for Celia Rudge...the fire wasn't her fault... the onlookers said the fire looked as though it had started in the chimney...but the fact that she ran away made it look bad on her."

"Yes, she was a good nurserymaid for the twins...couldn't do enough for them. Her husband was always a nasty piece of work, mind you..." Cook sucked her cheeks in as she reminisced. "Five years...do you remember, Mrs Williams? It was five years before Mr and Mrs DeVere could bring themselves to go into Chalsworth town again after that night."

"We've finished!" Sally clapped her hands and Penelope hopped up and down with excitement.

"This is the best Christmas ever," Dulcie said with a happy sigh.

"Eggnog and spiced apple juice all round," Cook cried, putting the bad memories out of her mind.

The rest of the evening passed in a whirl of activity as Florence and Sally helped Cook prepare the mountain of vegetables they needed for the next few days and Penelope and Dulcie dusted and polished until every piece of furniture in the house gleamed.

As Florence sank into bed at midnight she felt exhausted. The winter moon cast a silvery glow through her window and she tossed and turned, with sleep eluding her. Her mind drifted back over what Cook and Mrs Moore had been talking about until finally, she drifted off into a half-state of hovering between being asleep and awake.

Celia Rudge was the nurserymaid when they had the fire...looking after Miles and Hugo...Josiah Rudge was a bitter man, filled with hatred for the DeVere family...

The dreams and images pushed through her head, each one more fanciful than the last. Suddenly she sat bolt upright in her bed with a gasp. A terrible thought had just occurred to her.

"It can't be...surely not?" Florence's voice was croaky with emotion as she considered the outlandish idea which had forced its way into her mind and wouldn't let go.

"I have to find out..." She kicked the covers off

and scrambled to get dressed as quickly as she could, tiptoeing down the stairs as she swung her cloak over her shoulders.

"Tom, Tom, wake up." Florence shook Tom Sawley's shoulders urgently.

"Mhhhm? What is it?" Tom rubbed the sleep from his eyes, blinking in the light from her lamp. His hair stood up in every direction and he looked startled when he realised it was Florence leaning over him in his narrow bed in the hayloft over the stables.

"I need you to saddle up Bluebell. I have to go to Chalsworth right away."

Tom sat up. "What, now?" He peered past her looking out of the window at the inky sky. "It's not even dawn yet, can't it wait?"

"No, I have to go now. That way I can be back before anyone misses me." Florence tightened her shawl. "I wouldn't ask if it wasn't important, Tom. I'll make sure you don't get into any trouble, I promise."

Ten minutes later, Bluebell kicked up her heels and trotted towards Chalsworth at a brisk pace, enjoying the unexpected outing with Florence on her back. The sky was just starting to lighten over the Eastern horizon and Florence urged her into a steady canter, hanging on tightly to the reins. Low hanging branches whipped at her hood and several times she thought she was going to come a cropper, but as they pounded through the lanes, she gradually got the feel of Bluebell's pace and relaxed into the saddle.

The sound of Bluebell's hooves was muffled on the snowy cobbles and the only people who saw them rushing through the streets of Chalsworth were too busy going about their business to wonder who she was.

"Stay here, girl, I won't be long." Florence hitched Bluebell's reins over the railings at the end of Etnam Lane and hoped that she would still be there when she returned.

"Hunter, wake up!" She hammered on the green door, not caring if it woke the neighbours. This was too important to worry about such trivialities.

"Florence? What on earth are you doing here?" Hunter pulled her into the house with a smile. Her cheeks were flushed rosy pink from the cold night air and he thought she had never looked so beautiful.

"I need to speak to your mother. Is she here?"

Florence paced back and forth, twisting the ends of her shawl in her hands.

"I thought you'd be back, maid. You're a bright girl…"

Hunter looked startled as his mother edged into the room. She crossed her arms defensively and sank onto the nearest chair.

"I need to ask you a question Mrs Rudge…I beg of you…please answer it truthfully."

Celia Rudge nodded reluctantly and the tension around her eyes gave away her anxiety as she glanced in Hunter's direction. "Before you ask…I want you to know that I love my children more than life itself. Things ain't always been easy with Josiah…you have to understand that…"

Florence stood in front of the meagre fire and took a deep breath. "Mrs Rudge…Celia…is it true that you were the nursery maid for Mrs DeVere when Miles and Hugo were babies?"

"Y…yes, I was." Celia's hands trembled slightly and she put them in her lap.

"And…is it true that…" Florence gave Hunter an agonised look before continuing. "Is it true that your son Hunter is in fact Hugo DeVere? That you stole him to raise as your own son, on the night of the fire?"

"What?" Hunter's eyes rounded in shock and the blood drained from his face.

"I...I never meant..." Celia's face crumpled and tears rolled down her cheeks. "I'm sorry Hunter...I never meant to...Josiah was so angry with Mr DeVere...he swore blind he would find a way to get his revenge."

The clock ticked quietly on the mantelshelf and Hunter rushed to his mother's side as she sobbed into her shawl. "Josiah started the fire...he told me it was just meant to give the DeVere family a fright." Celia closed her eyes, remembering how the flames had licked up the curtains and devoured everything in their path, greedily sucking the air from the room. "It took hold so fast, there was nothing I could do to stop it. And he made me take you, Hunter. He said that if Mr DeVere could sack him from his job at the mill in such a heartless way, he deserved to lose something as well."

Celia sobbed again and took a shuddering breath. "That's why he sent you out picking pockets when you were nothing but a young boy. Josiah was rotten to the core...I wish I'd never married him...and we didn't have children of our own...not until much later when I had Elsie and Mavis." Celia's voice cracked with emotion as she recounted her terrible deed. "Josiah made you go out and earn the money that he was too lazy to do." She looked at Florence and shook her head. "I knew you'd end up guessing, one day. That's why I tried to stop you seeing Hunter...and why I tried to stop Hunter working for Miles."

Fresh sobs shook Celia's thin shoulders. "Josiah said if I didn't do his bidding...he...he said he would tie my hands together and throw me in the river."

"How did you guess?" Hunter's expression was dazed as he turned to face Florence.

"Cook and Mrs Moore mentioned that your ma was Mrs DeVere's nurserymaid. And then it all made sense when I remembered seeing the scar on your side when I came here yesterday. That was from the fire, I assume?" Florence looked at Celia who nodded mutely. "And the way that you don't look anything like Elsie and Mavis...or Josiah for that matter. When I saw you and Miles working together at the old mill, there was just something about the two of you. You both seemed so similar but I couldn't put my finger on why." She reached out and stroked Hunter's hand. "There was one other thing too."

"I can't believe all of this...what else was it?" Hunter asked quickly.

"I knew deep in my heart that you're not like Josiah. I've seen the sort of man he is, and I know you're nothing like him, Hunter. You're a kind and decent man...not like that monster."

"What will happen to me now?" Celia wrapped her arms around herself and rocked in her chair. "I'll be thrown into jail and the girls won't have a mother anymore. And you, Hunter? You'll probably never speak to me again for doing such a wicked thing?"

"No, Ma. I'll always love you, no matter who I am. You've done the best you could for me all these years. It's Pa who should pay for this. And he should pay for every time he's hit you and made your life a misery." Hunter sprang up and his jaw clenched with anger. "I'm not a boy anymore. It's time I stood up to that bully once and for all...for all our sakes."

Suddenly there was a scuffling sound at the door and it creaked open. Josiah Rudge stood on the threshold, swaying slightly. "I saw that lumpen old horse of yours tied up on the railings," he said pointing at Florence. "All she's good for is the knackers." He belched loudly and shuffled into the room, falling heavily into the armchair by the fire.

"I wasn't expecting you back Josiah. Shall I make you some porridge?" Celia plucked nervously at her hair, pulling it forwards to try and cover her tear-stained cheeks.

"What's she doing here, son? Is she yer fancy woman? Not enough meat on her bones for my liking."

Josiah chuckled at his own wit. The small room had quickly filled with the stench of stale beer that seeped from his pores and his words were slurred.

"That's all you can do, isn't it." Hunter's lip curled with distaste. "Insult people and demean them. You've done it to Ma all these years, putting her down, no matter how hard she worked, or what she did for you all those years ago..." His words hung in the air between them, like a challenge.

"What do you mean?" Josiah licked his lips and his bloodshot eyes darted furtively at his wife.

"I know everything," Hunter shot back at him. "Florence worked it out and Ma has finally told me. The fire...what you asked Ma to do for you... who I really am." His fists clenched at his side and Florence laid her hand on his arm.

"I knew you were no good from the moment I laid eyes on you." Josiah scrambled unsteadily to his feet and spat on the floor between himself and Florence. "Sticking your nose into things that are none of your business. Nothing this woman says is true," he added, gesturing in Celia's direction. "She's been nothing but a thorn in my side since the day I met her."

"That's not fair, Josiah! I've always tried to do my best for you."

"Pah, call that your best. Two whining girls for children, and complaining every time I lost a job... none of it was my fault."

Florence felt Hunter's muscles tense under her hand and stepped between them. "What you asked your wife to do was unforgivable, Mr Rudge."

His eyes took on a sly expression. "You can't prove any of this. Nobody would believe Celia...I mean just look at her...a pathetic scrap of shrivelled old woman, mumbling about ridiculous notions that are all in her head. I should send her packing to the mental asylum, that's all she's good for."

Hunter suddenly sprang forward and grabbed his father by the shoulders. "You'll have me to deal with if you lay one finger on Ma, from now on. Or

Elsie and Mavis. We've all had enough of your idleness and bad temper. I should have stood up to you long ago."

"Idle? I wanted a strapping lad to do my bidding, but what did I end up with? A daydreamer, always fussing around Celia and the girls making sure they're alright. You're a pathetic excuse for a man if you ask me."

Celia gave a hollow laugh. "He's more of a man than you'll ever be, Josiah."

"Is that right?" he snarled, glaring at her.

"You drink every penny you earn, and you can't hold down a job for more than a few days because of your temper. What have you ever given us? We'd be better off without you."

Josiah smashed his fist on the table, sending the cups rolling onto the floor where they smashed into sharp shards. "I won't listen to your whining and nagging for one more day, woman."

"Well you won't need to when you're in Gloucester prison for what you did to the DeVere family," Celia cried bitterly.

"Never! I'm not going to pay for that...they deserved everything they got. I've had it with all of you. I'm leaving and you can fend for yourselves. You'll soon be wishing I was back." He grabbed the jug from the mantelshelf and emptied the pennies from inside into his hand.

"Good riddance," Celia said, with a note of hysteria in her voice. "Don't think I'll take you back when you sober up and come to your senses, begging for forgiveness. We don't need you and we never will."

"Don't bother trying to find me," Josiah spat back. "If anyone's going to take the blame for what happened, it can be you, Celia." He barged past them and stepped back out into the snowy street, stumbling away as fast as his feet would carry him.

After a stunned silence, Celia rubbed her hands slowly on her arms and blinked as though she was waking up from a bad dream. "Do you think he's really gone?" she whispered.

"Only time will tell, Ma. But I hope so."

FLORENCE TIGHTENED HER SHAWL, seeing that the sky was getting lighter outside. "I have to return to Bisley Court before I'm missed." She stood on her tiptoes and kissed Hunter on his cheek, feeling her heart melt with love for him. "I have to tell the DeVeres, Hunter. They need to know that you're alive and well. I...I'm going to tell Miles first and then he can tell his parents. It's the right thing to do."

Hunter nodded as Celia started crying again. "I have to look after Ma. I can't let her take the blame for this. We have to let the truth come out and see what happens...the DeVere family might want nothing to do with me...but I can't turn my back on Ma and my sisters." He crushed her into a sudden embrace and pressed a kiss on her lips before standing back with a glint of humour in his eyes. "Thank you, Florence. I knew the moment I saw you at the Summer Fayre that there was something special about you."

om ran out of the stables as soon as he heard the hoofbeat of Bluebell's canter approaching and grasped her reins so Florence could dismount. "A quick rub down and a bucket of oats and nobody will be any the wiser," he said with a wink, leading the mare away.

"Thank you, Tom, I won't forget that you've helped me." Florence ran through the kitchen garden and burst through the door, just as Mrs Moore was taking the first sip of her morning tea, standing next to the table next to Cook.

"Goodness me, what are you doing up so early...and in your outdoor clothes. I hope you haven't been gadding about with one of the boys from the village?" Mrs Moore pursed her lips and drew herself up to her full height. "I thought better of you Florence, I'm very disappointed—"

"It's not what you think, I promise." Florence grabbed Cook and span her around. "This is going to be the best Christmas you've had for a very long time...I'll explain more later." She pulled her shawl off and quickly undid her cloak, throwing them over the back of the nearest chair. "Something incredible has happened..." she giggled and hugged Cook again.

"Well, blow me down...I don't know what's got into you Florence, but that's the last time we'll be giving any of the maids eggnog if this is what it leads to. You're quite giddy with it..."

Mrs Moore was left open-mouthed with surprise as Florence hugged her too before darting out of the kitchen and running towards the back stairs.

"Miles...Miles, are you awake?" Florence burst into his bedroom and wrenched the curtains back, flooding the room with light.

"Did I miss something? Is it Christmas day already?" Miles sat up and swung his legs out of bed, wriggling into his dressing gown. "Must you be so noisy and exuberant this early in the morning, Florence?" He yawned and strolled to look out of the window.

"I've got something to tell you...I think you should stay sitting down."

Miles picked up on the seriousness of Florence's tone and gave her his full attention. "What is it? Is something wrong at the old mill?"

"I've found your brother, Miles." Her words tumbled over each other as she tried to get them out. "I've found Hugo and he's alive and well...he's been living in Chalsworth all this time...and you've already met him...Hunter is Hugo...Hunter is your long lost brother, Miles...he didn't die in the fire...he was taken."

Miles gaped at her with incredulity. "Are you sure, Florence? You mustn't joke about such things. Hugo died in the fire, that's what I've always been told." He stood in front of her, grasping her shoulders as hope and disappointment chased across his face. "It can't be true. Whoever is telling you this must be an imposter."

Florence gave a shaky laugh and shook her head. "It's true, I swear on my life, Miles. Why would I lie about something like this? It's a long story, and if I tell you, you must promise not to judge Hunter's ma harshly...I mean his adoptive ma. She had no choice in the matter...I truly believe that."

Over the next few minutes, Florence explained everything that had happened as Miles listened without interrupting her. As she came to the end of her explanation, he took his handkerchief out and blew his nose loudly, holding back his tears of joy. "I can't believe it," he whispered. "All this time, my very own twin brother was just a few short miles away."

"I...I think I should tell your parents now." Florence stood up again, feeling a mixture of joy and trepidation. She had no idea how Mr and Mrs DeVere would respond to the news and prayed that they would take it well.

"We'll do it together, Miles said firmly. He took her hand and they hurried to the dining room where Sally was just serving porridge with winter fruit compote.

"Mama...Papa...we have some incredible news." Miles broke into a broad grin as his parents looked at him curiously.

"Oh no, not another harebrained idea...can't we get the chocolate factory up and running first?" Robert was in fine spirits and chuckled at his own joke.

"What is it, dear?" Evelyn replied absent-mindedly.

"Florence has found Hugo," Miles cried, his eyes shining with unshed tears. "He was taken in the fire and he's been living in Chalsworth all this time. The best thing is, it's Hunter. I've already met him and we got along so well...now I know why."

Evelyn gasped and dropped her cup of tea, not even noticing as it smashed on the floor by her feet. Her face had turned chalky white and her hands trembled violently. "My boy is alive? Hugo... my darling boy is alive?" Her words were a hoarse whisper and she looked at Robert with an agonised expression of longing, desperate for it to be true.

"Stop...stop. I won't have you spreading these wicked lies and upsetting my family." Robert jumped up, sending his chair teetering over backwards behind him. He strode forwards and grasped Florence, pushing her roughly towards the door.

"It's true, Mr DeVere. I'm telling you the truth." Florence gave him a beseeching look.

"You're to leave Bisley Court immediately. Don't pack your things, and you won't receive any pay, I want you gone within ten minutes and I never want to see you again. My dear son...died...

they never found him and my wife and I have had to live with this grief for twenty years..." Mr DeVere's voice cracked with emotion and Florence struggled to free herself.

Suddenly she realised she had nothing left to lose. She had to make herself understood, and never mind the consequences.

"You've been blinded by bitterness, Mr DeVere. Ever since I've been here, I've seen the way you treat Miles as though he's a disappointment. But I can tell you, Miles is a wonderful man...you're lucky to have him as a son. And as for Hunter...he didn't do any of the damage in the old mill, it was his father. Hunter is a kind and caring person who had a terrible start in life through no fault of his own."

"How dare you." Mr DeVere looked towards Miles and shook his head. "It's not true..."

The words poured from Florence's mouth as though she was powerless to stop them. "Both of your sons are good people...I'm sure they must get that from you, Mr DeVere. Would you really close your heart to your son right when you've found him again, simply because you don't want to believe in what's right under your nose? A man in your position could do so much good for others...

if you just had the faith and courage to be a better person."

She gave Mrs DeVere a searching look, seeing that her eyes were shining with hope. "You gave me the opportunity of a better life when you offered me a job here and I'm forever grateful. Hunter is your long lost son, I promise. Please just give him a chance and I'll never bother you again." With that she turned and ran from the dining room, knowing that her time at Bisley Court had come to an end and she would be all alone again. Her feet carried her towards the kitchen and she felt the searing sense of loss as she entered its homely surroundings. She knew she would have to explain everything to Cook. What should have been a happy day had turned into a tragedy.

"I'm sorry, Mrs Williams. I want nothing more than to stay here working with you, but Mr DeVere has said I must leave immediately."

In the kitchen, Cook gave Florence a floury embrace before looking into her eyes. "Are you sure it's not just a spat that will blow over? Mr DeVere can be a bit hot-headed at times. Surely he's grateful for what you've done." Her eyes filled with tears again. "I can scarcely believe Hugo was alive all this time. That poor bonnie baby, taken from his twin brother." She dabbed a handkerchief on her cheeks, laughing and crying at the same time.

"I can't stay. I don't think even Miles can save me this time. I've never seen Mr DeVere so angry...but I promise I'm telling the truth—"

Suddenly the door from the kitchen garden burst open and Tom darted in, yanking his cap off his head and trampling straw onto the flagstones.

"Sorry, Cook...Florence...there's a man here to see you. He says it's urgent." He grabbed Florence's hand and dragged her down the steps, pulling her along the path to the front of the house. "He said you have to see him, no matter what," he panted, propelling Florence through the gate and out onto the sweeping driveway.

Hunter steadied the thoroughbred horse that was wheeling under him, before jumping off and handing the reins to Tom. The horse was lathered in sweat from the gallop from town and Tom quickly led him away, calming him with his soothing words.

"I had to come, Florence. I've wanted to say this for a very long time." He strode over to her and stopped, looking deep into her eyes. He took her hands in his and pulled her closer. "Florence May, will you marry me?"

"I...but—" Florence felt as though all the air had been sucked from her lungs. She had yearned for this moment for so long, but it had come too late.

Seeing her confusion, Hunter brushed his fingers against her cheek and looked away with regret in his eyes. "I know I've done things I'm not proud of in the past. I'm sorry if I've spoken out of turn." He sighed. "You deserve only the best, Florence, and I can see I'm not the man you'd hoped for. But I had to tell you how I feel and ask you...even if you say no."

"No," she replied hastily. "It's not you that's in the wrong. It's me...I've been thrown out of Bisley Court. Mr DeVere didn't believe what I told him... and Mrs DeVere is upset...I've made a complete mess of everything. Why on earth would you want to marry someone like me? I have no home and no job. I'm a lost cause."

Hunter smiled and shook his head. "You're the most amazing girl...woman...I've ever met, Florence. I don't care about whether you have a job, or what the DeVeres think of you. All I care about is not letting you slip through my fingers and regretting it for the rest of my life." He looked down into her deep brown eyes, drinking in every contour of her face. "So can I ask you again? Will you marry me, Florence?"

"Yes, Hunter. I would love nothing more than to be your wife." Florence gazed up at him and melted into his arms as he pulled her into an embrace. She could feel their hearts beating in unison as the snowflakes drifted down and knew that she had never been happier than in that moment.

"Thank you, my love. I'll always take care of you." Hunter's deep voice rumbled in his chest and he bent his head.

Their lips met in a passionate kiss and Florence could feel all her worries ebbing away, knowing that they were meant to be together, ever since that fateful day at the Summer Fayre all those years ago. No matter what the future held, she would love this man until the day she died.

* * *

"WHY ARE YOU STILL HERE? I told you to leave…and take this…this imposter with you." Mr DeVere's angry shout split the air, sending the birds clattering up from the trees in fright.

Florence sprang back from Hunter, but he held tight to her hand, not wanting to let her go even for a moment.

Mrs DeVere pushed past her husband and ran down the steps, not caring about the snow swirling over them. "Hugo? Is it really you? My darling boy…can this miracle be true that you're alive?" Her eyes filled with tears and she stood in front of Hunter not knowing what to do.

"Don't Evelyn. Don't encourage them. We lost our boy in the fire and we have to accept it." Mr DeVere's words came out as a strangled croak as he joined his wife, trying to pull her away.

"Mother? Father? I don't know what to call you…but what Florence told you is true. I have the scars to prove it." Hunter shrugged his coat off and wrenched his shirt up, showing them the puckered skin over his ribs. "The man who I thought was my father…Josiah Rudge…he's to blame. He started the fire and forced my mother to steal me from you because he wanted a son who he could send out to work. Josiah is a scoundrel…but he's left our lives forever. He'll never darken our door again… he's too much of a coward. So now it's just me looking after Ma and my two sisters, which is for the best, trust me."

"It can't be true, Evelyn. Don't fall for this fanciful story." Mr DeVere looked more closely at Hunter and for the first time, Florence could hear doubt mingled with hope in his tone. "Surely not... not after this long?"

"Papa, I know it's true. You have to believe them." Miles appeared behind them at the top of the steps, clutching a large picture. "Look, I knew there was something familiar about Hunter when he came to work at the old mill, but I couldn't think what it was."

Miles navigated the icy steps carefully, using only one stick. "Remember this old oil painting of Grandpapa as a young man? I used to see it every day when it was hanging in the old nursery at the top of the house and I'd all but forgotten about it." He turned the painting around and Florence gasped. The likeness to Hunter was uncanny. "See, Hunter looks exactly like Grandpapa did at that age. You always said we looked different as babies, Mama, but you can't deny the resemblance between us, even though we're not identical."

Evelyn and Robert looked at the painting and then back at Hunter, their faces suffused with joy. "It really is...it's a miracle, it is you Hugo."Evelyn threw her arms around Hunter and sobbed with happiness.

"I...I...don't know what to say." Robert blinked rapidly and looked at the ground for a moment as he gathered his thoughts.

"Say welcome home, silly," Evelyn said, with a broad smile. "Our family is whole again."

Miles handed the painting to Mrs Williams who had come to see what all the commotion was and extended his hand to shake hands with Hunter. "Welcome to Bisley Court, old fellow. Now...at long last I'll have the brother I always dreamt of having...someone to beat at chess and go for a pint of beer with." He chuckled as Hunter hugged him, clapping him on the back.

"Someone to help you with all your crazy ideas, you mean," Hunter laughed.

The mellow chimes from the grandfather clock pealed from the hallway and Mrs DeVere looked up at all the staff who had gathered at the top of the steps. Cook was crying into the corner of her apron as Vernon Sawley put his arm around her to comfort her, and Mrs Williams had the broadest smile she had ever seen as she stood looking between Miles and his brother.

"Cook, can you lay up the table for five for

luncheon, please? It's Christmas Eve and we have Hugo and his delightful new wife-to-be joining us." She turned to smile at Hunter and Florence. "If you'd like to of course?"

Florence flushed pink and Miles winked at her. "I knew you two were well-suited. I'm glad my brother had the gumption to propose to you."

Mr DeVere cleared his throat and looked sheepishly at his wife. "I owe you an apology, Florence. Evelyn always says I need to think before I speak…something I once told you to do as well I believe," he added with a wry smile. "I'd be very happy to welcome you to our family, with our son, Hugo. You've given us the best gift ever and I'll never forget your bravery and honesty to find out the truth for us."

Florence felt as though her heart would burst with happiness as they walked into the hallway of Bisley Court. The candles on the Christmas tree twinkled in the shadows and the pine cones on the fire filled the air with the scent of winter.

"I want to know everything about you," Mrs DeVere said, taking Hunter's hand. "And I haven't forgotten about your mother, Celia. You must invite her and your sisters to visit us as soon as possible."

"She's very worried that you might seek some sort of retribution," Hunter replied, suddenly serious. "Although I'm happy to be part of the DeVere family, I can't turn my back on Ma, and Elsie and Mavis. I've given them my solemn promise that I will always take care of them, no matter what happens."

Mrs DeVere paused and looked at her husband before speaking. "Robert and I will honour your promise, won't we dear?" He nodded with a grateful smile. "Robert knew Josiah from days of old and even back then we knew he was an unsavoury fellow, that's why I offered Celia the job of nursery maid. I could see she needed work and I hoped she might manage to squirrel away a few coins from her pay, in case he ever abandoned her. As long as Josiah has gone, I think we can agree that Celia was only doing her best to survive in difficult circumstances. If we can't find it in our hearts to forgive her at Christmas, when can we?"

Hunter linked hands with Florence as they walked towards the dining room, and for a brief moment, it felt as though only the two of them existed. He pulled her closer. "Thank you for giving us all the best gift ever, my darling future wife," he said as his mouth curved into a smile.

"My wishes came true," Florence replied with a chuckle. "Even without that lucky button that you gave me. It's a good job you were there to pick me up and dust me down that day, even if you did look like a mischievous sort of boy I should have walked away from."

"I'm very glad you didn't," Hunter whispered. "Besides, I was already falling in love with you then, even though you were covered in dust, and I always will love you, my sweet." He tucked her hand into the crook of his arm and stopped under the mistletoe that Sally had hung up in the hallway.

"Shall we?" Hunter murmured, glancing upwards with a glint in his eye.

Florence laughed. "You have my heart already... I suppose another kiss won't harm." She stood on her tiptoes and brushed her lips against his, feeling every nerve in her body tingle with delight. "Happy Christmas, Hunter," she murmured against his lips. "And I wish...for a long and wonderful life by your side."

"Come along, you two." Miles peered back out from the dining room. "Mama is already asking when the wedding might be. Two family weddings in one year. I think that deserves a toast, don't you?"

EPILOGUE,

Three Years Later...

"What do you think about this for the curtains, Florence?" Dulcie struggled through the doorway with a pile of material in her arms that was so tall she could scarcely see over the top.

"Dulcie! Put those down immediately." Florence jumped up and relieved her friend from the load she was carrying. "Norman said you were supposed to be resting."

"It's weeks until the baby is due. Besides, I want to see the gatehouse finished as much as you do." Dulcie sat on the nearest chair and rubbed her swollen stomach absentmindedly.

"Well at least have a cup of tea before we start work." Florence poured the tea out and cut her a slice of cake.

"I still expect to see Mrs Sherringham walking in," Dulcie said, glancing at the door. "Although she loves her new home in Chalsworth. I've heard that Mr Jerome has taken to calling on her most days since she moved there and she told me the new dress I'm making for her is to wear at the Summer Fayre. There's to be a cream tea at the vicarage and Mr Jerome said he would like her to help him."

Florence smiled as she sipped her tea. "I think she would make a good vicar's wife. She was always very kind to you, helping you set up your dressmaking business."

"I know," Dulcie agreed. "Norman always says it was a blessing that I ended up working for her." She took a bite of Florence's poppy seed cake and her eyes suddenly sparkled with mischief. "You'll never guess who came in for a new dress fitting the other day?"

"Hmmm…Mrs Collier?"

"No, it was Matron Ebworth." Dulcie chuckled. "Of course she's getting on a bit now but she recognised me."

"What did she say?" Florence's eyes rounded as she remembered the spartan office and the way Matron couldn't wait to be rid of them.

Dulcie sighed. "She was actually quite polite… almost apologetic. For a moment I wanted to remind her how she'd told us we wouldn't amount to anything. But I decided to be the better person and just said that the dark blue calico would suit her well."

"You always were more diplomatic than me," Florence chuckled. "I would have told her that it was her words that spurred us on to try and do better in life, just to prove her wrong. Remember that dreadful old coal shed and the rats scuttling in the dark?" She shuddered at the memory and looked around at the homely room they were sitting in now, grateful for the comforting glow it gave her.

"We did alright, didn't we Florrie?" Dulcie used the old nickname she had called Florence when they were children and Florence blinked back her tears.

"More than alright, Dulcie. You married your wonderful Norman, and you have your first baby on the way. Plus you've got your dressmaking business and women come from miles around for you to make a dress for them."

"And you brought happiness to the DeVere family, Florence. Of all the incredible things you've achieved since we left the orphanage, that's the most miraculous one. I'm so proud of you...of both of us."

Florence sighed happily and nodded. "It hasn't been without its hiccups," she confided. "I think Mr DeVere blamed himself for the fire for all those years because he had sacked Josiah Rudge. Miles told me that he apologised to him not long after we found out that Hunter was really Hugo. He felt so guilty about being hard on Miles...he said he daren't allow himself to feel too close to him in case he lost Miles as well, from his ill health. He buried himself in work and grew more distant from Miles, even though he loved him all along."

Dulcie dabbed a handkerchief at her eyes. "Oh Florence, did Robert really say that?" She sniffed again. "This pregnancy makes me cry at the slightest thing, but I'm so happy for Miles that he and his father made their peace. And what about Hunter...I mean Hugo—"

"Did I hear my name?" The door suddenly burst open and Hugo walked in, followed by two infants crawling behind him in a determined fashion.

"Hello, my love, did you manage to wear the terrible two out?" Florence laughed as her husband rolled his eyes.

"Chance would be a fine thing. I swear it's more exhausting having Alfie and Rose for an hour than spending a whole day overseeing things at Thruppley Mill. How you manage is quite beyond me, although you always were a force to be reckoned with."

"I can't believe you ended up having twins as well, Florence." Dulcie watched as the toddlers used the edge of Florence's chair to haul themselves up and stood swaying on their chubby legs. Rose had Florence's dark eyes and Alfie looked the spitting image of Hugo.

"It took us by surprise as well," Florence said, stroking their silky curls. "But we wouldn't change a thing, would we." She darted Hugo a look of adoration and he bent to brush a kiss on her lips.

"Miles has asked us to go for dinner tomorrow night. Mother and Father are down from London for a few weeks and they want to see us all. I said yes, if that's alright."

"Of course it is, silly. You don't have to check with me." Florence pulled Rose onto her lap. "Dulcie and I are just deciding on what material to have for the curtains and then everything will be finished for the gatehouse."

"You didn't mind living here, instead of the main house?" Dulcie asked curiously.

Hugo chuckled. "This house suits us perfectly, doesn't it Florence." He smiled as his wife nodded because she had asked him the same questions once. "I might be a DeVere but I would have found Bisley Court overwhelming. Compared to where I grew up, the gatehouse is like a palace. I have everything I want here, and more."

"The big house is much better suited to Miles and Cora," Florence added. "I would have found it far too strange living as the lady of the house after being a maid there. It's wonderful that Hugo and Miles live close enough that they can make up for all that lost time, though. And it means that Alfie and Rose get to see their two cousins almost every day."

Dulcie stood up and brushed the creases from her dress. "Right, let's make a start measuring up for your curtains then. Mr Sawley is taking me back to Chalsworth shortly and Norman will send a search party out if I'm late. He's on tenterhooks now that the baby is nearly here." She smiled fondly at how attentive her husband was being. Florence had been very wise all those years ago to engineer things for her and Norman to keep crossing paths. That was why they had already asked her to be godmother to the baby, which Florence had accepted with delight.

The following evening, Hugo and Florence walked along the sweeping driveway to Bisley

Court, arm in arm. Celia, Elsie and Mavis had arrived earlier in the day to take care of the twins and Florence had persuaded them to stay with them for a few days longer.

"Do you think your ma will ever get used to coming here?" Florence asked Hugo. She looked up at his handsome profile against the evening sun and smiled.

"I think she will, in time. She felt so bad about what she did that she was terrified to meet Mother and Father, even though I told her they bore her no grudge." Hugo paused to watch as a swan followed by three cygnets glided serenely across the lake.

"I think it was a good idea to help her move to a different house in Chalsworth," Florence replied. "There were too many bad memories at the old house on Etnam Lane, and now that Josiah is out of your lives they deserved a fresh start."

"Let's hope he never returns," Hugo muttered with a slight shiver.

"He wouldn't have the gall." Florence squeezed his hand to reassure him. "Anyway, Celia isn't that same terrified woman anymore. She's got more grit than most people think. She would probably send him packing if he dared show his face again, not that I think he would," she added hastily.

"I'm glad that Ma is getting to know Mother better now. I overheard them talking about Miles and me last time Mother visited. What we were both like as little boys. They sounded happy, and it seems we were both very similar."

"Well of course," Florence chuckled. "You only have to see you and Miles together now to see how similar you are. And your ma deserves her happiness after everything she suffered from Josiah. She adores helping Dulcie with the dressmaking, and Elsie and Mavis are getting an education. You've all left that part of your lives behind now, my love."

Hugo turned and took Florence in his arms, looking deeply into her eyes. "Sometimes I wonder if this is all a dream," he said softly. "If it hadn't been for your bravery, coming to tell me what you did, everything could have ended so differently."

Florence grinned up at him. "Well everyone kept telling me I spoke my mind too much... Matron...Mr Collier...Mr DeVere...even you." She laughed and brushed a lock of hair back from Hugo's forehead. "At least when it really mattered, I managed to speak my mind without getting into trouble for once."

Hugo shook his head and they walked briskly up the steps into Bisley Court where Miles and Cora were waiting for them.

"Come along, you two. Papa and Mama can't wait to see you again. I told them they need to come down from London more often, but now that Papa is in Parliament I'm not sure if they'll be able to."

Florence held Hugo's hand as they strolled down the hallway into the dining room. Even though she hadn't been a maid there for three years, she was still glad of Hugo's solid presence at her side when the occasional moment of self-doubt crept back that the other maids might think badly of her for marrying a DeVere.

"It's their problem if they do," Miles had assured her when she had mentioned it to him once. "We all think of you as one of the family now, Florence. It doesn't matter that you came from lowly beginnings. Times are changing and if people look down their noses at you...well, they'll have me to answer to."

"How are you my dears?" Evelyn bustled forward and swept Florence and Hugo into an effusive embrace. "You both look as if you're blossoming and Cora tells me that the gatehouse reno-

vation is almost complete. I can't wait to come and
see what you've done."

Florence accepted the small glass of fruit cup
that Robert handed her and chatted with Evelyn
and Cora while the men talked business in front of
the fire.

"Dinner is served, Sir." Mr Middleton creaked
into the room, followed by Sally who was carrying a
tureen of soup and Penelope who had the bread rolls.

"Hello, Florence. How are the nippers?" Penelope gave her a broad grin, then giggled as Sally
nudged her to remember her manners.

"They're fine thank you, and it's lovely to see
you both. Sally, I hear a wedding is on the cards
soon?" Sally blushed and nodded happily. "I'm glad
to hear it," Florence replied.

As they ate their soup, Robert cleared his throat
and took a sip of his sherry. "Now that we're all
gathered, Evelyn and I have a small announcement
to make."

Hugo reached for Florence's hand under the
table and squeezed it. He had already hinted that
his father had news, but he had refused to tell her
what it was, saying he wanted it to be a surprise.

"I've been talking to Cora's father, Gordon and

we have decided that it's time to make some changes with our factories, to make life better for the people who work for us."

Miles caught Hugo's eye and they shared a smile.

"We are going to build new cottages for the workers, both for Thruppley Mill and for the Chocolate factory. It's like you said to me once Miles, if it weren't for them, we wouldn't be who we are as a family. We owe it to them to give them better living conditions and to make their lives more pleasant. I've finally come to the conclusion that a happier workforce can only be a good thing for us all."

"That sounds wonderful, Robert," Florence said quickly and Cora nodded enthusiastically. "You'll be setting a wonderful example to the other factory owners too. Bravo."

Robert smiled at Florence and then at Cora. "I'm glad you both agree because I'm hoping that my delightful daughters in law will be involved."

"We want you to help design the cottages, Florence, and you too Cora, if you'll agree," Evelyn chimed in. "You have a unique insight into life at the mill, Florence. We thought it would be nice to have parks, a bowling green, a lake, even a library. What do you think?"

Florence's eyes lit up and she looked up at Hugo, stunned by the invitation. "If you think—"

"I think you would be perfect at the role," Hugo nodded with a broad smile.

"Do say yes, Florence, Cora has already said she would like to be involved. We can make a real difference to our workers' lives." Miles reached for Cora's hand and they both looked at her.

"I'd be delighted," Florence said happily.

Suddenly there was a commotion at the door and Mrs Moore bustled in. "Florence, would you mind stepping out for a moment, Mr Sawley has some news for you."

Florence jumped up and hurried to the front door with Hugo right behind her. Vernon Sawley was twisting his cap in his hands and his face was creased with worry, making Florence's heart sink. "What is it? Is there a problem at home?"

"No miss. I just came to tell you that Dulcie's time has come and I was worried that I drove the carriage a bit roughly yesterday." He gulped nervously, then broke into a wide smile. "I was in Chalsworth this afternoon and Norman saw me. He ran out of the shop and said to tell you they've had a little girl. She's called Florrie." His eyes misted slightly and he gave Florence a nod of happiness before scurrying away to the stables.

"She named her baby after you," Hugo said softly. He took Florence in his arms and they stood at the top of the steps looking out across the rolling fields towards their home in the distance. Florence leaned her head against his chest, overcome with emotion.

"You've inspired so many people in your life. I'm a lucky man to be able to call you my wife," Hugo added. He held her gaze and then bent his head, kissing her passionately.

"We're both incredibly blessed, Hugo. And that's not the only thing. You're going to need even more energy in a few months' time."

Hugo looked puzzled. "You mean you want to do more refurbishments to the gatehouse? I mean, you're welcome to of course, but I thought you liked—"

"I do, but we'll need to get another bedroom ready," Florence interrupted with a grin, glancing down at the slight swell of her belly.

"You're expecting another baby?" Hugo looked at her with shock and delight as Florence nodded.

"Yes, our beautiful little family is going to be

even more special soon. Maybe you need to sit down again, to get over the surprise?"

"Not before I've had a kiss from the most wonderful woman I've ever known."

Hugo drew Florence into his arms again and she melted into his embrace, feeling his heart beat against hers. His lips caressed hers as the evening sun sank behind the distant horizon and Florence knew their love would last forever, just as she had secretly wished for, all those years ago.

*** The End ***

READ MORE

If you enjoyed The Maid's Winter Wish, you'll love Daisy Carter's other Victorian Romance Saga Stories:

The Locksmith's Dilemma:

Lily Palmer is used to keeping secrets to stay one step ahead of poverty. But with secrets come difficult choices. Will Lily make the right decision, or risk losing everyone she cares for?

When Lily's mother sees a way to secure her place in high society she jumps at the chance. But a terrible accident leaves the two of them practically destitute and it falls to Lily to save them from ending up on the streets.

In a twist of fate, Lily finds herself in a new position as a housemaid to Horace Dryden, the renowned locksmith favoured by the wealthiest in society.

A tragedy in Horace's past means he offers her an opportunity, and for the first time in her life Lily has the chance to make something of herself.

But her new role brings her to the attention of the wrong people and Lily soon finds herself facing dangerous choices with far-reaching consequences.

Her friends Chester and Oliver are the only people she can confide in. But with the threat of violence hanging over her, Lily is forced to do something that could put them all in danger.

Just when she thinks she's made the right decision, an even worse fate comes knocking at her door to jeopardise her future happiness.

Will Lily stay one step ahead of the betrayal she's sucked into, and keep her promise to look after the people who rely on her?

And dare she hope that the man she loves will forgive her when he finds out what she's done, so her dreams of happiness can come true?

* * *

Do you love FREE BOOKS? Download Daisy's <u>FREE</u> book now:

The May Blossom Orphan

Clementine Morris thought life had finally dealt her a kinder hand when her aunt rescued her from the orphanage. But happiness quickly turns to fear when she realises her uncle has shocking plans for her to earn more money.

As the net draws in, a terrifying accident at the docks sparks an unlikely new friendship with kindly warehouse lad, Joe Sawbridge.

Follow Clemmie and Joe through the dangers of the London docks, to find out whether help comes in the nick of time, in this heart-warming Victorian romance story.